# 1
# SUGAR CREEK GANG
# *The* SWAMP ROBBER

## Paul Hutchens

**MOODY PUBLISHERS**
CHICAGO

All Scripture quotations are taken from the *New American
Standard Bible,* © 1960, 1962, 1963, 1968, 1971, 1972,
1973, 1975, 1977, and 1994 by The Lockman Foundation,
La Habra, Calif. Used by permission.

Original Title: *The Sugar Creek Gang*

ISBN: 0-8024-7005-X
ISBN-13: 978-0-8024-7005-8
Printed by Bethany Press in Bloomington, MN – 2/2015

We hope you enjoy this book from Moody Publishers.
Our goal is to provide high-quality, thought-provoking
books and products that connect truth to your real needs
and challenges. For more information on other books
and products written and produced from a biblical per-
spective, go to www.moodypublishers.com or write to:

Moody Publishers
820 N. LaSalle Boulevard
Chicago, IL 60610

19 20 18

*Printed in the United States of America*

# PREFACE

Hi—from a member of the Sugar Creek Gang!

It's just that I don't know which one I am. When I was good, I was Little Jim. When I did bad things—well, sometimes I was Bill Collins or even mischievous Poetry.

You see, I am the daughter of Paul Hutchens, and I spent many an hour listening to him read his manuscript as far as he had written it that particular day. I went along to the north woods of Minnesota, to Colorado, and to the various other places he would go to find something different for the Gang to do.

Now the years have passed—more than fifty, actually. My father is in heaven, but the Gang goes on. All thirty-six books are still in print and now are being updated for today's readers with input from my five children, who also span the decades from the '50s to the '70s.

The real Sugar Creek is in Indiana, and my father and his six brothers were the original Gang. But the idea of the books and their ministry were and are the Lord's. It is He who keeps the Gang going.

PAULINE HUTCHENS WILSON

# The *Sugar Creek Gang* Series:

# 1

It was the laziest day I ever saw and so hot it would have made any boy want to go fishing or swimming—or maybe both. I don't think I was ever so glad in my life that school was out, because just as soon as I saw those big fat fishing worms being turned up by Dad's plow when he was breaking the garden, I knew what I wanted to do. What I *had* to do, in fact, or the whole day would be spoiled.

Right away I laid my rake down—I was raking the yard—and went out behind our garage to a barrelful of empty tin cans that we'd pretty soon have to haul away to the dump down along Sugar Creek. I threw a handful of dirt into a can and started dropping in the biggest, juiciest worms I could find—the kind that would make any fish go so crazy with hunger he'd risk getting caught rather than let the worm wriggle around on the hook all by itself.

It made me think of that time I sneaked into Mom's pantry and filled my pockets full of cookies, and had my mouth full too, just as Mom came hurrying down from upstairs where she'd been making the beds. She took one look at me, called out sharply, "William Jasper Collins!" and made a dive for me. She caught me too and—but that's a story I don't tell anybody. I was just little then and didn't know any better, but after that I made up my mind I'd never take any more cookies without asking first.

I've got the best mom in the world, don't think I haven't. I guess punishing me hurt her worse than it did me. That night when I'd said my prayers and been tucked into bed, she hugged me awfully tight.

But as I said, that was when I was little, not more than seven years old. Now I say my prayers by myself, climb into bed in the dark, and just call, "Good night!" down the stairs. I wouldn't let Mom know for all the world that I kind of miss being tucked in, but I do.

Well, pretty soon I had that bait can almost full of worms. I was thinking how hot it was here in the garden and how cool it would be down at the river and how Roy Gilbert and I would just lie there in the new green grass and watch the lazy specks of foam floating along on the water. And every now and then our bobbers would start acting funny, moving around in circles and ducking under the water like tiny diving birds, and our string of fish would get longer and longer with rock bass and chub and—

*"Jasper!"*

Dad's big voice was just like a finger being poked into a great big beautiful soap bubble. It burst my dream all to nothing. And when Dad called me Jasper instead of Bill, I knew he didn't like what I was doing.

I set the bait can down in the deep furrow and answered innocently, "What?"

"What are you up to?" he demanded roughly. He had the horse's reins slipped around his shoulders, and his hands were gripping the plow handles real tight. I could tell, because his sleeves were rolled up and the muscles on his arms were like great big ropes. My dad was awful strong—or maybe I should say *very* strong. My folks are having a hard time teaching me to use the right words. It's awful hard to quit using the wrong ones, you know.

I didn't know what to say to my dad. So I just called back indifferently, "Nothing," and picked up a clod of dirt to throw at a blackbird that was gobbling up some of the worms I had missed.

"Come here!" Dad said, "and bring that can of worms with you!"

My heart went *flop*. I couldn't fool Dad in anything, and I knew better than to try. But I could see the whole day being spoiled. Just think of all those fish swimming around on the bottom of the creek, hungry for nice, wriggling worms. And just think of how Dad liked to eat fish when they were all cleaned and rolled in cornmeal and fried crisp and brown the way Mom can fry them. I decided to remind him how good fish would taste for supper that night. I picked up the can and walked across the garden to where he was waiting.

Dad could always read my mind just like I could read a book. (I was in the fifth grade in school, you know.) He had turned around and was sitting on the crosspiece between the plow handles. His big brownish-red eyebrows were down. I stood there holding the can of worms in both hands.

The horses were so hot that white lather was all over them. They'd been sweating so much there was lather where the harness rubbed their sides, and you could smell the sweat. Sweat was trickling down Dad's face too. I guess there never had been a hotter spring day. Little heat waves were dancing all over the garden.

I kept looking down at my toes, which were digging themselves into the cool, newly turned earth, and Dad kept glaring at my can of worms. I hadn't really done anything wrong, hadn't exactly planned or even thought anything wrong. Except maybe I was wishing I didn't have to rake the yard and was hating rakes, hoes, garden-making, and all the work. I guess you'd call it being lazy. Maybe it was.

"Well?" Dad demanded.

Then I saw his snow-white teeth gleaming under his red-brown mustache and the twinkle in his eye. It was like a cool dive into Sugar Creek on a smothering hot day. Whenever I saw Dad's teeth shining under his mustache, I knew everything was all right.

"Bill Collins," he said, and I felt better than ever—even though his voice was still gruff. "I want you to take that garden rake, clean it off, and put it away in the toolhouse. Then get your long cane fishing pole and go down to the river

—you and Roy Gilbert or some of the boys—and fish and fish and wade in the branch until you get over that terrible case of spring fever. And don't come back until you've caught all the fish that'll bite! You've had a hard school year—with your arithmetic, geography, and science—and you need a rest!"

At first I couldn't believe he meant it. But when he reached out, put his arm around my shoulder, gave me a half hug, and said, "I was a boy once too," I believed him without trying.

You should have seen me carry that long cane fishing pole in one hand and the can of worms in the other, running straight toward the river where I knew Roy'd be waiting for me. For the night before we'd laid our plans to meet there at two o'clock, if we could.

But I never dreamed so many things could happen all in one day, or that before I'd get back home again Roy and I would have been scared almost to death, or that this was going to be the beginning of the most exciting week of my whole life.

# 2

It happened this way. Roy and I were lying there in the grass on the bank of the creek just as I told you we would. Our fishing poles reached far out over the water, and funny-looking, enormous-eyed, four-winged dragonflies nosed around the lines like hummingbirds around Mom's morning glories.

All of a sudden my bobber, which was nothing more than a big cork out of Mom's vinegar jug, started acting as if it was alive. It moved around in a funny little half circle, kind of slow at first, and then *plunk!* Just like that, it ducked under, making a big splash. The end of my pole bent down and struck the water with a smack. I knew that I'd hooked a fish.

I grabbed my end of the pole and held on tight. Roy told me afterward that my eyes stuck out like a dragonfly's when I was pulling that fish in. And my line didn't break either, because I had a brand new one.

That's another reason I knew my dad liked me, maybe better than any dad ever liked his boy before. When I'd gone to get my fishing pole out of the toolshed an hour before, it had a brand new line on it with a reel and everything. Dad acted surprised when he saw it, but there was a twinkle in his gray eyes. And I knew he'd bought it for me.

Maybe you think I wasn't scared enough when my bare feet slipped on the edge of the bank and flew right out from under me and I went down *kersplash* into the water. But I still was holding onto that fishing pole for dear life.

Roy was standing on shore, jumping up and down, yelling at the top of his lungs, and screaming at me what to do and not to let go of the pole. "I saw him!" he cried. "He was a big black bass two feet long!"

I could barely touch the bottom of the creek with my feet. While I was feeling the heavy pulling and jerking of that fish on the end of the line —and thinking about my new overalls being all wet and what Mom would say when I got home —Roy got hold of one of my hands and started to pull me out.

"Give me the pole, quick!" he screamed.

And then, just as it had happened to me, it happened to him. His feet slipped, and there we were, both of us in the water. Of course, we could both swim, so there wasn't any danger of drowning. You know, everybody ought to learn how to swim when he's little because you can never tell when you'll need to know.

Well, between the two of us we landed the fish. It was a black bass, all right, only it was about fourteen inches long—or maybe twelve —instead of two feet. And that's how Roy came to get the nickname "Dragonfly." His eyes were bigger than his head! He was always seeing things twice as big as they were. He kind of liked the name, and so did I. I felt quite proud that I'd thought of it first.

But I tell you, that water felt good!

"Now that we're all wet, we'd just as well go swimming," Dragonfly said. "Besides, we'll have to let our clothes dry, won't we? And they'll dry quicker than anything hanging out on those bushes while we swim."

Dad hadn't told me I *couldn't* go swimming. I guess he figured maybe I'd like to, and he didn't want me to be tempted to disobey him. Dragonfly's parents hadn't told him not to either.

So in about a minute and a half we had that twelve-inch bass—oh, well, maybe he was only eleven inches long—fastened on a stringer and swimming around in his jail over in the branch that empties into the creek right near where we'd been fishing. Our clothes were hanging on some bushes drying, and we were out there in that fine, clean water, splashing, swimming, diving, and having the time of our lives. Understand, we were waiting for our clothes to dry. We weren't just swimming for the fun of it, of course!

We stayed in for maybe a half hour, having a grand time and wishing all the gang was there. Let me tell you about our gang, the finest bunch of boys you ever heard of. I reckon there will never be a gang of boys in the whole world that'll have any more fun than we did.

There was little Jimmy Foote, who was the littlest one of us and who always obeyed his parents and was a sort of mascot for us because he was so likable. And he wasn't any sissy either! That little fellow was brave! Once when there was a rifle—but that's another story, which I can't tell you till a little later.

Well, there were Little Jim and Poetry and —but let me tell you about Leslie Thompson. We called him "Poetry" because he was always quoting a verse or two of poetry. Everything he saw would start him off, and sometimes we'd have to shut him up or the rest of us wouldn't get a chance to say a word. He was almost as broad as he was tall, and his voice was changing so that it sounded squawky. He used to sing soprano in the junior choir in our church, but now he wouldn't sing at all. And folks just don't seem to understand that when a boy's voice gets all squawky like a duck with a bad cold, he's terribly bashful about singing in public. It didn't mean that Poetry was any less interested in church.

I know because once I stayed all night at his house, and before we went to bed he got right down on his knees and prayed. And when he got through saying his little poem prayer, which he'd learned when he was little, he added a lot of words of his own, just like he was talking to somebody right in the room. And I guess he was. It kind of scared me at first, but I didn't let him see the stubborn tear that got in my eyes about that time. Anyway, that's how I learned to add things to my memorized prayer too.

Poetry was always acting mysterious. He was

going to be a detective someday, he said. And he was always getting into mischief.

And then there was Circus Browne, whose real name was Daniel August Browne. Whatever his parents wanted to give him such a long-legged name for, I don't know. We called him "Circus" because he was so acrobatic. He could turn handsprings, walk on his hands, and shinny up a tree quicker than anybody I ever saw.

Then, besides Dragonfly, Poetry, Little Jim, Circus, and me, there was Big Jim. We called him Big Jim because he and Little Jim had the same name and we didn't want to get them mixed up. Big Jim was the leader of the gang, and he knew all the things a leader ought to know. He'd belonged to a Boy Scout patrol before he moved into our neighborhood and was what they call a first class Scout. First he'd been a tenderfoot, then second class, then first class. He could have gone on to qualify for star or life or eagle rank, but his folks had had to move, and there wasn't any Scout troop where we lived. Besides, you have to be twelve years old to be even a tenderfoot. That meant that Dragonfly, Poetry, Little Jim, and I would have been left out. So Big Jim just called us The Gang.

Big Jim was strong, almost as strong as my dad, I reckon, and he used almost perfect English. He could make a tourniquet for stopping the flow of blood when anybody was bleeding terribly. He could tie twenty-one different kinds of knots, such as the fisherman's bend, the half hitch, and the bowline. He was the catcher of our ball team and could knock in more home runs than any of us. He could jump the farthest and was the best fighter I ever saw—except we didn't get into many fights because Big Jim kept the other boys in the neighborhood from starting anything. They were all scared of him.

So Poetry could quote more rhymes than any of us. Circus could climb a tree the fastest and do more acrobatic stunts. Dragonfly was able to see the farthest. Little Jim acted more like a Christian should than all the rest of us put together. And Big Jim was our leader. As for me, I guess I was just an ordinary boy. I didn't even have a nickname except just plain Bill, which is short for William.

As I said, Dragonfly and I must have stayed in the water for about a half hour. Anyway, when you haven't been in swimming for a long time and it's such a terribly hot day, time goes pretty fast. You forget about everything except how much fun you're having.

It was Dragonfly who saw it first—saw *him*, rather. All of a sudden he stopped splashing and yelling and muttered to me, "Quick, Bill! Get down under the water! Somebody's comin'."

We both dropped down so that only our chins and noses were sticking out, looking maybe like a couple of turtles with only their noses showing above the water.

"It's an old man with long white whiskers," Dragonfly whispered, "and he's coming right straight this way."

I peeked. "I don't see anything," I said. And

then I saw him—a short man, round like a barrel, bareheaded, with whiskers and long, shaggy white hair that reached down to his belt. Except that he didn't have on any belt, on account of he was wearing a pair of old overalls. He had on dark glasses, and he shuffled along as though he couldn't see very well.

He looked just like the people we call tramps sometimes look. "Itinerants," Dad calls them, which doesn't sound so bad. But I guess there never was a boy who wasn't a little bit scared of one that looked as fierce as that one did.

# 3

We kept as quiet as we could, hoping the old man wouldn't see us and would go right on past. We didn't want him to take our fishing poles or our bass or—

"Look!" Dragonfly pinched me so hard under the water that I nearly yelled. But the fact is, I was so scared I couldn't have yelled very loud, for I'd never seen such a fierce-looking man in my life.

"He's spied our clothes!" Dragonfly said.

Sure enough, he had, and he was pushing his way through the tall weeds straight toward them!

We knew right then we'd better do something quick, for I had a brand new knife in my overalls pocket, and Dragonfly had a watch in his.

"Let's scream like a hundred wild Indians," Dragonfly said, his teeth chattering.

It sounded like a good idea, so we both let out a yell as loud as we could, making it sound as fierce as if we were a whole tribe. Except that I knew it must have sounded like two kids, half scared to death, which we were.

But the old man didn't even look around. He acted as if he was deaf. Now he was standing right where our clothes were hanging, and in a second he was going through our pockets. He found Dragonfly's watch first and held it up in the sunlight, close to his big dark glasses. Then he brushed it against his long white whiskers, put it to his ear and listened, then shook his head as if he couldn't hear a thing.

"My—my *watch!*" Dragonfly gulped.

I'd never seen him so scared before. And being scared is kind of like getting the measles —it's catching. Dragonfly's face made me afraid too. But if getting scared is contagious, so is getting angry. Pretty soon we were both so mad I knew we were going to do *something* in just about a minute.

We yelled again, a wild, bloodcurdling scream. But do you think that made any difference? Not a bit!

"He's deaf!" Dragonfly said.

I believed it. And when I saw my new knife going into the old man's pocket, I got madder than ever. Then the old man just naturally picked up our clothes, slung them over his shoulder, and waddled back through the tall grass and weeds whistling. *Whistling,* mind you!

We knew we couldn't go home without our clothes, though at that time I didn't think much about anything because I was so mad.

And so was Dragonfly. We would have to do something, and you can bet your life we did. We climbed up that creek bank, picked up a couple of clubs, and whooped it up, yelling, "Come back here with our clothes! Stop, or we'll shoot!" and about everything frightening we could think of.

This time that barrel of a man, with his long white hair shining in the sunlight, turned around and glared at us. He seemed to know the lay of the land there too, for he shuffled quickly to the left and tossed our clothes right over into the middle of a brier patch and said gruffly, "Help yourself!"

*Brier patch!* Why, we'd be scratched half to death trying to get those clothes!

That was too much. We both made a dive for him, and before you could say Jack Robinson we'd caught up with him—not because we could run faster but because he stumbled and fell and rolled down the hill. We stumbled over the man and landed right on top of him, getting our arms and legs all tangled up like an octopus doing an acrobatic stunt.

"Stop!" he cried. "Don't hurt me! I'll give up!" And then, as if he was crazy, he started quoting poetry:

> "Jack and Jill went up the hill
> To fetch a pail of water;
> Jack fell down and broke his crown,
> And Jill came tumbling after."

In a jiffy those long whiskers were off. And the long hair. And the dark glasses. And we were looking straight into the mischievous blue eyes of Leslie "Poetry" Thompson, who started to laugh as loud as he could and quoted from "The Night Before Christmas":

"He had a broad face and a little round belly,
  That shook when he laughed,
    like a bowl full of jelly."

Poetry sprang to his feet and began to dance a jig and to sing:

"Hey, diddle, diddle,
  The cat and the fiddle,
    The cow jumped over the moon.
The little dog laughed
To see such sport,
    And the dish ran away with the spoon."

He held up Dragonfly's watch and my knife and started all over again about the cat and the fiddle.

I was still mad, and so was Dragonfly. And as much as we liked good old mischievous Poetry, we made *him* wade into that brier patch and get our clothes, which were still a little wet.

Then we all went in swimming. Poetry got ducked again and again for being so smart. Only it was just like trying to duck a rubber barrel; he wouldn't stay under, and he could swim and dive like a fish.

"Where'd you get those whiskers?" I asked when we were dressing.

"And your dark glasses and your long hair?" Dragonfly added.

"Wouldn't you like to know?" Poetry asked. Then he lowered his voice and looked around mysteriously. "I found 'em," he said.

"Found 'em?" Dragonfly and I asked in chorus.

"In the old hollow sycamore tree down along the swamp."

"How do you suppose they got *there?*" I asked.

Poetry looked at me scornfully as if I was too ignorant to know much about mysterious things. "They grew there, just like moss," he said.

"Maybe there's some robber around here, and he used these for a disguise," Dragonfly said, trying on the dark glasses.

Poetry looked pretty serious when Dragonfly said that. And that, too, was like getting the measles. The more we thought about it, the more we began to wonder if Dragonfly might not be right.

That old sycamore was the biggest tree around here. Three or four feet from the ground was a big opening. Inside, it was all hollow and large enough for three of us boys to stand in it at the same time—that is, three the size of Little Jim and Dragonfly and me. Poetry couldn't even get inside.

The tree grew about fifteen feet from a steep rocky precipice that dropped straight down to Sugar Creek. It was an awful lonely place down in that part of the woods, and none of us boys ever went there alone because our folks didn't

want us to. But we sometimes went there together.

Somebody had started the rumor that the
old swamp was haunted, and that meant ghosts.
While none of us boys believed in ghosts, we
weren't exactly hoping to meet one without Big
Jim along, who could have made short work of
any ghost in a jiffy, he was so strong. But Poetry! You couldn't ever tell what he was going to
do next. And as I told you, he'd already made
up his mind he was going to be a detective
when he grew up, and he wasn't afraid of anything.

The three of us stood there sober-faced,
talking about what we'd better do. Each of us
tried on the disguise just to see how we looked
with it on. Then all of a sudden it was five
o'clock, and we knew we'd better be getting
home quick or our folks'd be worrying about
us. That was one of Big Jim's rules: we weren't
to cause our parents any worry if we could help
it.

Dragonfly made me take the fish even though
we had both caught it. Tomorrow, we decided,
we'd get Big Jim and Circus and Little Jim, and
the six of us would go down along the swamp
and investigate that old hollow tree.

We'd sneak up on the place and attack it
from ambush. Of course, there wasn't anything
to it . . . but you never could tell.

# 4

It felt mighty good to be carrying that fish home for Dad to see, although I kept wondering what Mom would say about my wrinkled overalls. They'd been pressed so nicely when I'd left the house.

But Mom was as good a mother as Dad was a father. She was standing in the kitchen doorway when I came up past the barn and garden carrying my black bass, the fishing pole, and the bait can.

Dad was washing his face and hands in the big washbasin under our grape arbor, which ran along the side of the garage. He straightened up with soapsuds all over his face and neck and looked me over from head to foot. His eyes lit up proudly when I held up the fish.

"It's wonderful," Dad said.

"They're terrible," Mom said.

Dad was looking at the fish, and Mom was looking at my soiled overalls.

I didn't have a chance to be either glad or sad, now, did I? But I was worried some just the same, because I didn't want to make Mom feel bad.

"I'll wash them myself," I said.

"He won't need washing," Dad said, "only

cleaning and skinning"—meaning the fish, of course, not me.

Just then the telephone rang, and Mom had to go answer it, so I had a minute to be happy about my fish. Dad brought a ruler and measured it. "Ten and one-half inches," he said. And he gave me the other half of that hug he'd started to give me earlier in the afternoon.

Supper was ready right away, and as soon as I had washed my face and hands and combed my hair, we sat down to eat. I was still feeling kind of heavy around the heart on account of my overalls, even though I was as cheerful as anything on the outside and as hungry as a bear on the inside.

Mom's big, soft brown eyes kept watching me.

We all bowed our heads quietly before eating. Hungry as I was, I kept my eyes shut all the time Dad was praying, which wasn't very long. Dad knew how hungry a boy could get at mealtime—and most anytime. He was a boy once himself. Oh, Dad was a real Christian all right. I knew that not only because he prayed and read the Bible and went to church but because he acted like one toward Mom and me and everybody else.

I was just itching to tell them the whole story about how I caught the fish—that is, how Dragonfly and I caught it. But I couldn't on account of not wanting Mom to know I fell in the creek.

But pretty soon, when she was waiting on

the table and pouring a second glass of milk for me, she reached down and kissed the top of my head just as though I was a little boy. And she whispered in my ear, "Don't worry, Billy boy, I know you didn't do it on purpose." Then she went around to her chair and sat down again. After that it was the easiest thing in the world to talk.

Dad laughed and laughed and wiped his eyes over Dragonfly and me falling into the water.

That night after I'd scrubbed my feet good and gone up to bed, calling, "Good night," at the top of the stairs, I stood beside my bed a long time before getting down on my knees to say my prayers. I looked out the window at the moonlight shining on the barn and the garage and the new garden. I could even see the little green tops of onions set in long rows across the garden.

Then I looked up at the Milky Way, stretched like a big white bow across the sky and at all the thousands of stars. And I just kind of felt that God had made them, and I couldn't help but be glad I had a dad and mom who loved Him and tried to teach me about Him. Somehow I couldn't help but think maybe He was like my mother and father, only more wonderful and a lot greater. He had made an awful pretty world, and He must have liked boys a lot because He'd sent His own Son down to earth to be a boy Himself once.

I knelt down and said my little poem prayer and then added some words of my own, which I can't remember now. I felt like telling Jesus I loved Him, the way I did my parents and maybe even more, but I was scared to. But I did love Him just the same. And I guess He can hear a boy's thoughts anyway, the same as his words. Only it's good to use real words when you can.

I tell you that nice clean bed felt good even if it was hot. The pillow was so big and soft, only . . . only . . . why, it was wet! No, not much, but as though someone had sprinkled a few drops of water on it.

And that's how I found out I'd been crying a little bit. I hadn't known it at all. I sighed a great big happy sigh, and the next thing I knew it was morning.

# 5

It was a fine morning. The big red sun was just peeping up over the horizon as if he wasn't quite awake yet and hated to get up. The birds were singing like everything. Right up in the top of our big walnut tree, which grew on the other side of the garden and where we had the biggest swing in the whole neighborhood and where the gang liked to play, was a robin hollering for all he was worth, "Jasper Collins! Get up, get up!" I liked robins, even if they did call me Jasper.

And down on the ground, with his head cocked to one side listening for a worm, was another robin redbreast standing in the sunlight. He must have heard a worm all right, for all of a sudden he turned like a flash and pulled at something with his big black-and-yellow bill. And, sure enough, in a second there was a big, long fishing worm in his beak, twisting and squirming like it was on a hook.

It really doesn't hurt fishing worms much to be put on a hook, Dad said once. Dad is a sort of a scientist-farmer, and he said something about its being just a "minor irritation." Kind of like a boy getting his neck and ears washed with soap and water when he'd rather wash them himself by swimming and diving in Sugar Creek.

Pretty soon that robin flew up into a fork of the walnut tree, where there was a nest full of little robin quadruplets waiting for their breakfast. Think of eating worms for breakfast! *Worms!*

I dressed in a hurry because today was to be the big day. Right after dinner, the gang would all get together, and Poetry would tell us what he'd found in the hollow tree down by the haunted swamp. We'd all arm ourselves with bows and arrows and slingshots and with a big club for Little Jim, and the fun would begin.

First thing, though, was getting through the morning, which would be awful long since all of us boys helped our folks in the morning. That was Big Jim's rule. I guess there never was a boy who liked to work unless he could imagine his work was play. But Mom had been trying to teach me ever since I was little that work came first and *then* play. I guess she was right. Besides, if you really love your parents, you like to do things that make them happy.

I helped Mom wipe the dishes, which most boys think is a girl's job, but it isn't when you don't have any girls in the family. I finished raking the lawn, built a fire, burned all the dead grass and leaves, and gathered up all the tin cans and things that somehow had gotten scattered all over the barnyard mainly because I'd been using them for imaginary golf balls. Then I dropped the potato slices with the eyes in them into the long, deep rows Dad had made across the garden. I stepped on them with my bare feet so they'd be pressed down into the dirt better and would grow quicker. Maybe you think that wasn't fun, feeling the cool, damp dirt oozing up between my toes!

And finally it was noon—dinnertime—and we had fish for dinner. "What kind of bait did you use to catch this bass?" Dad asked. And I said, between mouthfuls, having a hard time to eat slowly on account of having to meet the gang at one o'clock, "Why, just plain worms. Why?"

"I just wondered," Dad said. "I found a nice little chub on the inside of him." A chub is a small, carplike fish, you know. "And the little chub was full of fishing worms," Dad added.

I was surprised. That meant that first I'd hooked a little chub, and then the bigger bass had come along and had swallowed the chub. Right away I knew what kind of bait to use for bass the next time I wanted to catch one.

"It'll be all right to fish for bass today," Dad said. "If the game warden had seen you catch that one yesterday, it would have been too bad. You didn't know, but it wasn't bass season yet."

Well, at ten minutes to one I was ready to go down to the spring where the gang had agreed to meet. It was Thursday, and we always met there on Thursday afternoons, if we could.

I ran upstairs to get my binoculars, thinking maybe we'd need them. On the way down again I stopped to fasten the strap around my neck. Dad had the radio going, listening to the midday news, and all of a sudden I went numb all over. At just that minute I'd heard the announcer say, "Be warned to be on the lookout for a man suspected of being an accomplice in a bank holdup. It is believed he is hiding somewhere in the swamp."

I couldn't make out where in the swamp, because there was a lot of static on the radio.

"He's described as having black hair and eyes and . . ."

When I got downstairs and looked at myself in the mirror, I was as white as a sheet. But I hurried out of doors quickly so the folks wouldn't see me and ran as fast as I could through the woods toward the spring. My heart beat wildly because of what I'd heard and because it looked like maybe we were going to have a chance to help catch a real robber.

# 6

I was the first one of the gang to get to the spring, and Circus was the last. He'd had a hard time persuading his parents that it was important not to miss a meeting. Circus's folks—his dad especially—never did understand boys very well, although his dad must have been a boy once himself.

But sometimes grown-up people are funny that way. They forget that inside a boy there is something that just makes him want to keep his promise to the gang.

And I tell you, it's pretty hard to obey your parents when they don't understand. We had to, though. Big Jim said he'd read it in the Bible as plain as day—*"Children, obey your parents."* Little Jim agreed it was true; he had seen it in the Bible with his own eyes. "Besides," Big Jim said, "if you ever want to become a Boy Scout, one of the qualifications is obedience."

Well, pretty soon we were all there. Big Jim had come with a mysterious package under his arm. Circus climbed a small elm sapling almost as soon as he got there and was swaying in the top, back and forth, looking every bit like a monkey in the zoo. Dragonfly and Poetry and Little Jim and I started tumbling around in the grass like kittens having a good time. All six of us were as pleased to see each other as if we hadn't been together in years.

The spring, you know, comes bubbling up out of a hole in a rock at the bottom of a steep hill, only about twenty feet from the creek. Dad had had the water tested to see if it was all right to drink, and it was.

Just that minute a big green shitepoke came flying up the creek with his long neck sticking out in front of him like the long handle on my green coaster wagon. His wings were flapping and driving him through the air awful fast. He was the most idiotic-looking bird you ever saw.

I had just gotten my binoculars focused on him and was following him up the creek with my eyes when Poetry was reminded of a verse from *Hiawatha*. Away he went in his squawky voice. It was about as squawky as the big quoke heron's, which goes quoking up the creek at night sounding like a young rooster learning to crow:

"Then the Little Hiawatha
    Learned of every bird its language,
    Learned their names and all their secrets;
    How they built their nests in summer,
    How they hid themselves in winter;
    Talked with them whene'er he met them,
    Called them Hiawatha's chickens."

Poetry had finished the first verse and was starting the second when something came swinging down from above and landed right on top of him. Circus had caught hold of the top of the elm sapling where he was sitting and swung himself out. The top of the tree had bent right over to the ground and brought him down with it. When he let go, the treetop flew right back up again.

In another minute we were all trying it, each one climbing a tree and swinging from one to another or down to the ground, whichever we wanted to do. You can do that with elm trees, you know.

But all this was just wasting time, so pretty soon Poetry looked at me, and I looked at him. We decided to ask Big Jim to call the meeting to order so Poetry could show us what he'd found yesterday.

First though, Big Jim opened his package, and there was a whole packet of paper drinking cups. We knew right away what they were for. We'd studied in school about how everyone ought to have individual drinking cups for health reasons.

Big Jim picked up the old rusty cup that was sitting there on the rock and which everybody in the county had used for years maybe. We all stood solemnlike, wondering what he was going to do. First he held it up for us to see, and then he said dramatically, "You can never tell when someone is going to drink out of it— someone who has some terrible disease maybe —and then the next person who uses the cup may become infected."

Then Big Jim set the cup down on a rock,

and with another rock he pounded and hammered it until he'd smashed it all flat. Then he tossed it into the weeds, and pretty soon we had a sign up that said, "Please use paper drinking cups." When we were finished, the rest of the cups were fastened up on a tree by the spring in a little tin container just like you see sometimes in public places.

All of a sudden Poetry was gone, and then a minute later he came hobbling down the hill like an old man, with the long beard and long white hair and dark glasses on.

Dragonfly pinched me on the arm so hard I couldn't help but say, "Ouch," and then I shut up like a clam.

"Howdy, boys," Poetry said in the quavering voice of an old man. "Do you reckon maybe a feller can get a drink of water at the spring here?"

Little Jim looked as white as a sheet. Circus's monkey face was as sober as a funeral. I thought even Big Jim looked a little bit worried, for he was a boy even if he was our leader. He wasn't so much bigger than Poetry at that. Dragonfly and I were holding our hands over our mouths to keep from laughing.

"Where's my old rusty tin cup?" Poetry's voice quavered, and it didn't sound anymore like Poetry than anything.

But then Circus saw his bare feet and noticed how big and round he was. Two seconds later, Poetry was standing bareheaded and looking surprised and disgusted, and Circus was already trying the disguise on himself to see how he would look.

Well, Big Jim called a meeting, and Poetry, Dragonfly, and I told the others everything we knew, even to the radio announcement. Big Jim took it all pretty calmly, but I could see he was as much excited on the inside as the rest of us.

"Maybe I'd better run home and ask Mother if I can go," Little Jim said.

"Not much, you don't!" Circus said. "It's going to be a secret. Now, if you're afraid—"

"I'm *not* afraid!" Little Jim shouted bravely.

Of course, he was afraid, and so were all of us, but a boy likes to be scared a little bit. It feels good.

So pretty soon we were there, right down along the swamp, walking cautiously toward the old hollow sycamore tree.

# 7

It was Dragonfly who saw the man first, for, as I told you, he had the sharpest eyes of any of us.

"Psst!" he hissed. "There's a funny-looking man!" He dropped flat on the ground, which was a signal for all of us to do the same thing. It didn't do Poetry much good to lie down, though, because anybody couldn't help but see him.

There was a man all right, about twenty yards from the sycamore and walking straight toward it—or rather he was just walking along kind of lazylike but going toward the tree just the same. He was whistling a tune that sounded like "Old Black Joe."

Big Jim turned his face around toward us, raised a finger to his lips, and said, "Sh!" And his eyes said, "Don't you dare make a noise, any of you!" Then he handed the binoculars back to me. I noticed particularly that the man looked awful young to be a bank robber and that he had coal black hair.

When we'd all had a look with the binoculars, we knew that something was really mysterious, for the man was poking around inside the old tree.

"He's looking for something," Poetry said, maybe thinking of the whiskers and the glasses and the wig.

It's a good thing the grass was tall where we were, or the man might have seen us. For suddenly he stopped what he was doing and looked around quick as if he'd heard something. Then he walked away, following the creek and still whistling. Something must have scared him, though, for pretty soon he started to run for all he was worth.

I guess we lay there for maybe five minutes more, waiting for Big Jim to say we could get up. I could tell from the expression on his face that he was thinking hard. Then he said, "It won't do for us to act like we know anything special. Let's just get up and act natural like a bunch of boys having a good time."

Circus was about the only one of us that didn't have any trouble acting natural when he was trying to. He yawned, stretched, and said, "Boy, it feels good to lie here in the shade." Only there wasn't any shade there at all except what Poetry made.

So with all of us acting natural, or nearly so, we just moved along gang fashion until we got to the tree. Big Jim made us all stand back and keep on trying to act natural, which was pretty hard to do. We could hear him feeling around the hole in the tree with Little Jim's stick. Pretty soon he let out a low whistle, and I saw him shove something into his pocket and keep right on digging around. There was a strange look on his face when he came back to where we were.

Then all of a sudden there was a gunshot up the creek. Then another. And another!

It didn't take us long to get back to the spring, I can tell you, for that look on Big Jim's face and those gunshots scared us plenty. We were all so excited we could hardly talk, which was all right because we were supposed to do nothing but run anyway, which we did.

At the spring we sat down to rest, and Big Jim took a dirty brown envelope out of his pocket. He started to open it. And then we all jumped, for we could hear footsteps coming up along the top of the hill.

We sat there so tense we couldn't move. But then Big Jim shoved the envelope into his pocket and started whistling. Poetry rolled over on his side, yawned, and said, "Boy, I'm sleepy:

"In winter, I get up at night,
    And dress by yellow candlelight;
In summer, quite the other way
    I have to go to bed by day."

Little Jim slid over to Big Jim, and his right hand crept into Big Jim's hand, probably so he wouldn't feel so scared. Circus and Dragonfly started a wrestling match, and I took my binoculars and focused them on a snake that was swimming along in the creek.

The snake must have seen or heard us, for he ducked under the water and didn't come up again until he was almost all the way across and about ten feet farther down the creek.

All this time, the footsteps were coming nearer.

I guess we were all pretty relieved when we looked up and saw it was just my dad, with a big pail in his hand, coming for spring water. He stood looking at us, at our sign on the tree, and at the paper drinking cups. Then he filled his pail and said casual-like, "You'd better come home at five-thirty tonight, Bill. This is Thursday, you know."

You see, Thursday night is prayer meeting night in our church. Some kids might think it's kind of goofy to go to prayer meeting, but I didn't because I'd been going ever since I was old enough to be carried there. And when you've got a mother and father like mine, you think prayer meeting on Thursday night is all right. In fact, I felt sorry for Circus's folks. They didn't go any place on Thursday nights except to places where they shouldn't—Circus's dad especially. He was always getting drunk. Circus's mom really tried to be a good mother. They had several children, and all of them girls but one.

Circus's folks didn't know anything at all about the Bible. It didn't seem fair for a boy to have that kind of parents, but that's the kind Circus had. All he knew about the Bible was what he'd learned from Little Jim and Poetry and me, but mostly from Little Jim. Circus had quit swearing because Little Jim didn't like to hear it. Circus was the only one of our gang that did swear. And as quick as Circus knew it was wrong, he quit.

Just as my dad reached the top of the hill with his pail of water, he turned around and said without even sounding excited, "Maybe you boys would be interested to know that about twenty minutes ago the sheriff caught a boy bank robber down along the swamp. The robber is on his way to the hospital to get well of his wounds—they had to shoot him. And then it'll be jail."

Little Jim looked pale. When Dad was gone he said, "I hope he doesn't die without being sorry. Mother says unless a man repents of his sin and lets Jesus come into his heart before he dies, he won't *ever* be saved and can't go to heaven at all!"

After Little Jim said that, we all kept still for a minute, thinking different things. I wondered whether the bank robber's mother would go to jail to see him. How awful it would make her feel to have that kind of a boy. I wished every boy in the world had a mother like mine or Little Jim's or Poetry's. I bet there wouldn't be many bad boys in the world if they did.

We decided we'd better find a more secluded place than the spring before we opened that brown envelope. At the spring you can never tell when somebody's going to come for a drink. So we climbed to the top of a high hill over on the east side of the woods and stood around the big rock where we sometimes had our meetings. In a few minutes we were looking at a rough drawing of some kind with scrawly writing on it.

Right in the middle of the page was a bed that looked like a hospital bed, and in the bed was an old man with a nurse standing there holding a glass of water. The old man was saying, "More, please." Alongside the bed was a funny, crooked line, twisting along like a snake, and a little bird was in a tree close by, singing, "Sweet, sweet, sweet." There were letters and numbers and other lines running off from the one that looked like a snake.

"It doesn't make sense!" Poetry exclaimed.

It looked like he was right.

I kept watching Big Jim's face, for I knew he was thinking. Big Jim had the kindest face you ever saw, with clear blue eyes and a chin that had a big dimple right in the middle of it.

There wasn't any sense to my noticing the black fuzz on his upper lip when I should have been thinking about the map, or whatever it was supposed to be, unless it was because some people call other people's faces "maps." Anyway, I was thinking that Big Jim was old enough, almost, to begin shaving, and I envied his being that old. That little mustache meant that Big Jim was almost a man. I guess every boy can hardly wait until he gets to be a man.

Again it was Dragonfly who saw it first. Suddenly he was jumping up and down and hollering. "I've got it! I've got it!"

Big Jim shushed him up quick—all of us did, in fact.

"Look!" Dragonfly said, more quietly. "That nurse standing there means the old man is sick! He's asking for more water, and—and if you put *sick* and *more* together you have *syca-more!* It stands for that old tree!"

I guess we were all pretty excited right that minute, and we must have made a lot of noise because Big Jim said, "Calm down!"

Now that Dragonfly had seen it, it was as plain as day to the rest of us.

"And—and—and—" Dragonfly stuttered, "that snake crawling is a river. And the bird singing, 'Sweet, sweet, sweet,' means *Sugar Creek!*"

Figuring out that map was just like fitting together a jigsaw puzzle. Only it was harder. We were all sitting there on the rock now with the map spread out between us, racking our brains to decide what the other funny lines and words meant.

From the tree in the drawing there was an arrow with the number *20* written on it, pointing straight east—that is, if the directions on the map were the same as those on any ordinary map.

At the end of the arrow was the word *China*, and that didn't make any sense. Not until Little Jim said, quietlike, as if he was afraid somebody would make fun of his idea, "My daddy's brother is a missionary in China, and Daddy says China's right straight down through the center of the earth."

Without knowing it, he had solved the puzzle for us, for that meant go twenty feet east and dig straight down, and there we'd find whatever it was—the money, maybe, which had been stolen from the bank.

We all jumped up and started toward the sycamore tree with Big Jim in the lead. Having to go slow because Little Jim couldn't run as fast as the rest of us, we got there in about six minutes or a little more.

Well, there we were without a ruler or a tape measure, so how could we know how far twenty feet was without something to measure with? We weren't nearly as scared as we had been when we were at the sycamore the first time, since we knew the robber had been caught. But we were plenty excited.

"Somebody'll have to run home for a ruler or a tape measure," Big Jim said.

We all looked at each other. None of us wanted to go, knowing it was so near supper time that whoever went might not get to come back. His folks might not understand how important this was, and he couldn't tell them.

"Let's roll Poetry over seven times, and that'd make twenty-one feet 'cause he's three feet round," Circus suggested.

Poetry turned red and gave Circus a savage look. "I'm thirty-five inches," he said disgustedly, "and you wouldn't know your arithmetic well enough to divide twenty feet by thirty-five inches."

"I'm just four feet tall," Little Jim said.

In a jiffy he was lying down with his feet against the sycamore tree and with his body pointing straight east. Well, that looked like a good idea, so we just used Little Jim for a measuring stick, and soon we were what we supposed to be twenty feet from the tree. Poetry lay down and rolled over seven times too, just to show he was a good sport, and there wasn't much difference between the two measurements.

But we knew that somehow we'd figured wrong. All around, the grass was fresh and green, and nobody had ever buried anything there unless it was a long time ago. So maybe the map meant twenty yards instead of twenty feet?

Big Jim looked at his watch, then at me, and said, "It's five-thirty. We'll all have to go home to supper."

Of course, we felt pretty disappointed, but we agreed to meet again the next afternoon at one o'clock, if we could. Big Jim would bring along a fifty-foot tape measure, his father being a carpenter.

"I'll bring a gunnysack to put the money in," Little Jim volunteered.

We didn't laugh at him, because sometimes his ideas turned out to be all right.

# 8

Maybe I never told you that Poetry was my very best friend, but he was. When I got home and had helped Dad with the chores and we were eating supper, the phone rang. It was Poetry's parents, saying that if we'd like to, we could ride to church with them in their new car.

I was glad. That meant Poetry and I could sit together in church—that is, if we'd promise to be good and not get into mischief. But it would be a hard promise for any boy to keep—especially if he was sitting beside Poetry—even in church. His being mischievous didn't mean he was a bad boy, though. I knew he wasn't. Some boys are made different from others, I guess, and Poetry was that kind.

Right after supper, Dad had me drive the cows down the lane to the pasture. "Be sure to shut the gate and hook it good and tight," he called to me just as I left the barnyard with our five big Holstein milk cows.

"I will," I called back.

With a long stick, which I always used when I was driving the cows, I trudged along happily, thinking about tomorrow and wondering what we'd find or if the map had been drawn by some crazy person and didn't have anything to do with the bank robbery at all. That was about the oldest and dirtiest envelope I'd ever seen, and the map looked as if it had been drawn a hundred years ago—well, twenty years ago anyway, or maybe ten.

I heard Mom's voice calling me to hurry or we'd be late for church. When I got up close to the house, I heard her complaining a little to Dad, saying, "Whatever makes that boy so *irresponsible?*" or some such long word.

And Dad said, "He's a dreamer. He'll be all right if we give him time."

Pretty soon Poetry's family was there, and we were all in their car going up the road lickety-sizzle toward our church, which was maybe two miles from where we lived. We boys all lived out in the country in about the prettiest spot in the world, I reckon. Right across the road from the church, which was a country church, was a three-room schoolhouse. It wasn't the school we all went to—we had a little one-room school of our own right in our neighborhood.

It didn't take us long to get there. It wasn't even dark yet, and our car was the first one to drive into the big wide churchyard and park. Soon people came from all directions, and then the service began.

Poetry and I held the songbook together, and I noticed he didn't look at the page more than half the time. He just growled along, singing a sort of bass, knowing most of the words from memory, since he liked poetry so well.

The meeting wasn't exactly the kind to appeal to red-blooded boys like us. But we liked the music and the minister's prayer, which wasn't too long, and his sermon, which was easy to understand and wasn't too long either.

Then they had what they call testimonies, and different people stood up and said nice things about Jesus and how they loved Him and how their prayers were answered—things like that. I just sat kind of trembly on the inside because I loved Jesus too, maybe as much as any of them did. And I was wishing the minister would say, "Now if any of the boys and girls would like to say a word, we'll ask all the older people to keep still for a few minutes." But he didn't.

So I just sat there wishing I dared get up anyway, but I didn't, half promising myself I'd do it next Thursday night even if they didn't ask for boys and girls to. Hadn't Jesus died for boys and girls as well as for grown-ups? Even if I didn't know very much about it, I knew I loved Him anyway.

Poetry didn't get up either, he being bashful on account of his voice being squawky, although I reckon that wouldn't really have made any difference to the Lord if Poetry really loved Him.

Pretty soon, while the minister was talking again, Poetry and I almost jumped out of our seats when he said, "This afternoon I was called to the hospital to see a man who is supposed to be a bank robber. He was just a young man too.

Poor boy! He was all broken up about it, said he hadn't done anything wrong and was out there in the swamp looking for something."

Poetry's hand was gripping my arm so tight I could hardly keep from saying, "Ouch."

Then our minister asked us to pray for the man that he might be saved, because he wasn't sure the boy would ever get well—and even if he did get well, he ought to be saved anyway.

Poetry and I didn't pray out loud like some of the rest of them did, including my dad, but we prayed quietly anyway, even if our eyes were wide open. There wasn't anybody in the world that could pray better than my dad could, not even a minister. He prayed especially for that boy in the hospital. Then he prayed for all the boys in our neighborhood and for all the boys in the world, who, he said, would all grow up to be either good men or bad men, according to whether they became Christians when they were boys.

I guess Poetry must have felt like I did, because I saw him put his hand up to his eye quicklike and brush away something. I was thinking, *What if that boy had been one of the Sugar Creek Gang, or even Poetry or me?* Of course, he was eighteen years old, and I was only ten and Poetry about eleven or maybe almost twelve.

Well, the next morning my dad drove away in our car and was gone for about an hour and a half. When he came home, I saw him take his big black Bible out of the car and carry it into the house and lay it on the table. He said he'd been to the hospital to see Barry Boyland, which was the name of the robber—if he was one.

Dad was kind of happy too. "He's better," Dad said, "and the doctor thinks he'll get well in maybe a week or two."

"What else?" Mom asked.

"Even if he doesn't get well, it'll be all right," Dad told her, "because he took Christ into his heart this morning, and he's saved now."

Mom seemed awful glad to hear that. She liked boys and wanted them all to be saved. "And he wasn't a bank robber at all?" she asked.

"They don't know yet. He says he wasn't. Says he lived out in California, that his parents were dead, that he used to have an uncle that lived around here somewhere, and he had come to look him up. I asked him why he had been carrying a gun, and he said somebody told him there were bears up in the hills and he was afraid not to. And that when he saw the sheriff and his posse, he was so scared his gun accidentally discharged. They thought he was shooting at them, and because he had black hair like the robber was supposed to have had, they shot back at him.

"Just to prove he was really telling the truth," Dad went on, "he showed me a picture of his uncle, which he had with him, and I've brought it home for you to see."

Dad took out of his pocket a picture about the size of a postcard.

Mom gasped the way she did when she was terribly surprised and said, *"Old Man Paddler! Why—why—"*

"Let me see!" I said, getting there as quickly as I could.

"It's nothing," Dad said, not wanting to get me excited, I guess. "It's just the picture of an old man who used to live up in the hills but who disappeared about ten years ago when you were a little baby."

He handed the picture to me, and it was my turn to be surprised. In fact, I never was so surprised in my life before. The picture looked exactly like Poetry did when he had on the wig and long whiskers.

"What's the matter?" Dad asked.

"Nothing," I said. Then I added, "Did he really die ten years ago?"

"He must have," Dad said, "although nobody seems to know what became of him. That's his old cabin up in the hills—you've seen it—and people say it's haunted, maybe because nobody knows what happened to the old man. Anyway, I told Barry Boyland his uncle was dead, and he seemed very much disappointed."

You can guess that I, Bill Collins, was listening for all I was worth to what Dad was saying, and thinking and thinking and trying to figure things out. The way Dad described the robber, he was the same one we'd seen yesterday, feeling around in the old hollow tree. I kept thinking about the wig and the whiskers and the dark glasses that Poetry'd found and the funny map with the picture of the old man in bed. I thought maybe Barry's uncle was a crazy old hermit. Maybe he even drew the map himself, and maybe he hid it there in the old tree, and hid the disguise there too.

*But why?* I asked myself.

Anyway, maybe we boys would find out that afternoon. Now that we knew there wasn't anything particular to be afraid of, it would be like some new game, only a whole lot more mysterious.

Soon it was dinnertime, and right after that it was one o'clock. The gang was all down at the spring: Circus, Dragonfly, Poetry, Little Jim with his gunnysack, Big Jim with his tape measure, and me, Bill Collins.

First, I told them what Dad had said about the robber not being a robber at all and about him being saved. You should have heard Little Jim sigh with relief, just as if he'd been carrying something heavy for a long time and somebody had suddenly lifted it off his shoulders.

Even Circus seemed glad. There happened to be an elm sapling right there. He shinnied up it like a squirrel and stood on the first limb and slapped his hands against his legs like a rooster flapping his wings after he's just won a fight with another rooster. And then Circus crowed in a way that sounded exactly like our old red rooster at home.

We called a meeting and decided we'd start looking for the treasure, or whatever it was, right away. If we found it, we could help pay the hospital bill for Barry Boyland. You see, if he didn't have any parents, maybe he wouldn't have enough money to pay it himself. And if he *was* a robber—well, then, maybe we'd find the stolen money and get a reward. So pretty soon we were all there at the old tree again, measuring off twenty yards this time, which is the same as sixty feet, you know.

It looked like sixty feet was going to be right under the biggest wild rosebush of all, the one with the sharpest thorns. We measured all over again to be sure. As near as we could figure, going straight east, that was just where it was. And that meant that whatever was buried there, if anything, must have been buried before the rosebush started to grow a long time ago.

We just walked round and round, all of us being barefoot. We couldn't decide what to do.

And then Little Jim laid his gunnysack down right under the bush, laid himself down on top of it, and started raking away the leaves and dead grass with his stick. We knew he'd found something when we could hear the stick scraping on something hard.

Big Jim got excited then, and in a jiffy he was down there too, digging away with the woodsman's hatchet he'd brought along.

We were all pretty disappointed at what they found—nothing but a flat rock about a foot wide, all overgrown with moss and half buried in the earth. We stood there, looking at it and feeling spooky, for you could see as plain as day that it wasn't any ordinary rock. The fact is, it looked a little bit like an old-fashioned tombstone, like the kind we have in our church graveyard, only it was lying down, instead of standing up.

Big Jim was digging around it and was just about ready to pry it out and turn it over to see what was under it—or else what was written on the other side—when Dragonfly said, "Psst! Somebody's watching us! I saw him right over there in the bushes!"

I tell you, it didn't take Big Jim long to cover that stone with dead leaves and dried grass, or for all of us to start acting natural. Poetry was the first one to get started, having maybe a hundred poems tucked away in his mind somewhere. He dropped flat on the ground—anyway as flat as he could—and made a mournful face and with his hand up to his head said:

"Humpty Dumpty sat on a wall,
 Humpty Dumpty had a great fall.
 All the king's horses and all the king's men
 Couldn't put Humpty Dumpty together again."

Circus was already lying on his back, swinging his feet up and down, and saying, "One, two. One, two. One, two. Up, down. Up, down. *Whoa!*"

Big Jim crawled out from under the rosebush, rubbed his eyes, and scolded us for waking him up. He talked so loud and looked so fierce that for a minute we thought he meant it. Then he yawned and acted awful sleepy.

"Look, fellows!" I cried, holding up one of the roses I'd just picked, "Look at these pretty yellow stamens all around the green and white center! Why, this rose has only five petals!" I said surprisedlike. A stamen, you know, is the part of a flower that carries the pollen—if flowers didn't have them, you could plant a million seeds and none of them would grow.

But none of the boys were paying any attention to me, so I started looking for birds with my binoculars. In a moment I was looking at a big red-winged blackbird swinging in the top of a little tree along the creek, his scarlet shoulders shining in the sun.

I swung the binoculars around as though looking for more birds, and then I saw somebody, sure enough, right over in the bushes. And would you believe it! He was an old man with long white hair and whiskers, only he didn't have dark glasses on. Yes sir, he looked exactly like the picture I had seen of Old Man Paddler less than two hours ago.

I lowered my binoculars quick and looked around to see if Poetry was still with us, and he was.

Well, that meant we'd have to stop looking for the treasure now and wait till we were sure nobody was watching us. In fact, Big Jim said we'd better all go in swimming and come back later.

We were just starting to leave when the man came out from where he was hiding and began hobbling toward us, looking awful meanlike.

You could tell he was angry about something, for he waved his stick and shouted, "Get out of here! Don't you know this property belongs to me, you little rascals? Get out, I say! Run! Or I'll have the law on you!"

"It's Old Man Paddler!" I cried and started to run.

In a flash the whole gang was running helter-skelter through the woods, just as fast as we could go, and we didn't stop until we got to the spring. There we all dropped down on the grass and rested a minute so as to catch our breath and get cooled off before drinking. That's what you're supposed to do when you're hot, no matter how thirsty you are.

"Did you ever see a man so mad in your life?" Dragonfly asked.

"I never did," Circus said, filling one of the paper cups.

Of course, we'd all heard about Old Man Paddler living up in the hills a long time ago. We'd been up to his empty cabin two or three times. But he was supposed to be dead now. Everybody said so. Yet we'd seen him with our own eyes this afternoon, hadn't we? How can a man be dead and still be alive?

"Maybe we saw his ghost," Circus said. "My dad says this old swamp is haunted, but I never believed it before."

"There aren't any such things as ghosts," Little Jim said quickly, "'cause my mother says the Bible says that when a man's dead, he's dead for good, and that if he doesn't go to heaven, then he goes to that . . . that other place, and nobody ever comes back again."

Somehow I knew Little Jim was right, but I decided to ask Dad about it when I got home that night.

Anyway Big Jim still had the map. He said it probably belonged to the old man and we'd have to give it back to him. Maybe he had something buried there, and, after being away for ten years or more, he'd come back to get it.

We decided not to go back today but to keep the secret about the old man because we didn't want our folks to worry about us.

When I got home I had the grandest surprise waiting for me, and you'd never guess what it was.

"Let's hurry and get your chores done, Bill," Dad said. "You've been such a good boy that you may stay all night at the Thompsons, and you and Poetry can sleep out in their backyard in his tent."

Well, that was something I'd been wanting to do ever since school was out and Poetry had put up his tent! You can guess I didn't waste much time helping Dad with the chores, even if ordinarily I am kind of lazy about it.

# 9

Sleeping in that big canvas tent with Poetry was the most fun I'd had in a long time. It was what is called a "wall tent," about eight feet high in the center and four feet high at the side walls, and with a drop screen in front to keep out mosquitoes. Only there weren't many mosquitoes in our neighborhood because we boys, and my dad especially, had poured oil on the surface of all the ponds and puddles in the swamp. And also we were careful not to leave any water standing around in tin cans or kettles or things, because that's where mosquitoes breed.

You know, mosquitoes are funny things. The kind we have in our neighborhood are what Dad calls the Culex kind, which don't carry any disease such as malaria or yellow fever. Dad knows the scientific names for the kinds that do carry diseases, but they're too hard for me to pronounce, and I can't spell them anyway.

As I said, mosquitoes are crazy things— crazy looking and crazy acting. Did you ever see those little wrigglers swimming around in your folks' rain barrel or in a can of water?

Those ugly little "wiggle tails," as Little Jim calls them, are baby mosquitoes that have hatched out of eggs that their mothers laid in the water. Well, those little wrigglers keep growing and wriggling until they're as big as they'll ever get. And then all of a sudden they stop wriggling and float up to the surface of the water. They lie there just like they are dead until their skin bursts open all the way along the back and out crawls a full-grown mosquito. She flies away, all ready to stick her sharp nose into somebody— if she doesn't get slapped good and hard first. Say, does a mosquito bite ever itch! But if you put some soda water on it real quick, it'll feel a lot better right away.

My dad drove me over to Poetry's house and let me out at the front gate. "Be sure to be a good boy," he said, which I didn't like to hear because I'd heard it maybe a million times in my life already—a thousand times anyway. I guess maybe I needed it, though. Anyway, I wouldn't like it if my dad wanted me to be bad, would you?

So I called out cheerfully, "I will!" I was willing to promise most anything because Dad had been so good to let me stay all night with Poetry in his tent.

I carried my little brown suitcase proudly up the walk and around the house to where Poetry's tent was pitched under a big maple tree. Poetry was so glad to see me you would have thought he hadn't seen me for a whole year. He lifted up the drop screen at the front of the tent, which was made of what is called "bobbinet" and had a wide band of cheesecloth all around it for a border so it wouldn't tear so easy or wear out so quick.

Pretty soon we were inside, and was it grand! There were two cots, one on each side with an aisle about three feet wide between them. In a corner, Poetry had a nice little table with books and things on it—things such as a pocketknife, a compass, and his little black leather New Testament. Poetry was the kind of Christian who was brave and wasn't ashamed to let anybody know what he believed, while at the same time he was an honest-to-goodness boy that everybody liked. Maybe he was a little more mischievous than some boys, but I felt proud to have him as my best friend.

We decided to go outside.

"I'm glad you brought your binoculars," Poetry said, "'cause we might need them before morning." He didn't explain what he meant.

However, we used them right away, looking around at different things. By standing up on Poetry's chicken house I could look across the field and see the chimney of our house and the big green ivy vine that almost covered the whole south side. I could see the big window of my upstairs room, which I always kept open when I slept, even in winter. That was one of the reasons I had such good health.

All at once, while Poetry and I were still standing on their chicken house talking and thinking and liking each other awful well, Poetry's dad called out sharply from the barn, "Leslie Thompson! Get down off there right this minute! You're too heavy for that roof! Don't you know it might smash in and kill a half dozen of your mother's finest laying hens?"

"All right," Poetry called back and started to obey. "I only weigh a hundred and forty pounds," he said to me. "I guess my being so short makes me look like two hundred."

In a little while it was dark, so we told Poetry's folks good night and went inside the tent. Poetry took a match out of a waterproof matchbox, the kind everybody ought to have when camping. He struck it, and in an instant there was plenty of light to see to undress by, coming from a little kerosene lamp on the table in the corner.

We'd already washed our feet in an old foot tub just outside the tent door and had put on our slippers—Poetry's mom making sure we did it, so we wouldn't get her nice clean sheets all dirty.

When you're a boy, I guess nothing feels better than sleeping in a tent. We felt like real campers—or forest rangers! Pretty soon we had on our pajamas and were sitting on the edges of our cots, hating to turn out the light and crawl in. And I was wondering which one of us was going to say his prayers first.

Maybe Poetry was thinking the same thing, because finally he reached over, got his New Testament, handed it to me, and said, "Let's read our chapter together tonight."

I guess I forgot to tell you that Poetry and I had promised each other we'd read a chapter out of the Bible at least once each day and that we'd pray for each other every night.

Well, I turned to the book of Acts, which is the fifth book of the New Testament, and read about fifteen verses. It was the story about Paul and Silas having to go to jail for preaching the gospel and how they sang songs at midnight and were so happy because they loved Jesus in spite of being in jail with their feet all fastened tight in wooden clamps. Then there was a big earthquake, and the jailer tried to kill himself with a sword because he thought the prisoners had escaped. But instead, he became a Christian, and he and his whole family were baptized before morning.

It was a great story, I tell you, and we liked it a lot, especially since Poetry and I kind of liked each other the way Paul and Silas did. We made up our minds that if ever we had to go to jail for being Christians we'd do it, and we'd sing at midnight too, only we wouldn't exactly want any earthquake.

Then the two of us got down on our knees together beside Poetry's bed and said our prayers. This time Poetry didn't say his little poem prayer at all but just talked to the heavenly Father with his own words. He explained afterward that he was getting too big to just quote a poem to God, so he'd decided to talk to Him right out, knowing that He loved boys and that Jesus had been a boy once Himself.

Soon the light was out, and we were lying there on our cots, thinking and talking and telling each other stories and looking through the little square hole at the top of the tent entrance, which was open for fresh air.

I was looking out at the sky with the stars looking down at us as if they were our best friends, when Poetry started to say:

"Twinkle, twinkle, little star,
How I wonder what you are!
Up above the world so high,
Like a diamond in the sky."

I always did like that poem, ever since I was little, so I made him quote all of it, liking especially the verse that goes:

"In the dark blue sky you keep,
And often through my curtains peep;
For you never shut your eye,
Till the sun is in the sky."

Then we began to get sleepy, and in a minute we were gone.

Did you ever wonder where a boy goes when he goes to sleep? Of course, you don't really go anywhere. When you wake up, you're still right there in bed.

At least, I was when I was awakened a little later by the strangest noise coming from the old maple tree somewhere right above our heads. It sounded like somebody crying or else moaning or wailing in a trembly voice.

As soon as I was fully awake, I knew it was nothing but a screech owl and nothing to be afraid of. I'd seen plenty of them in the daytime. They generally sit all alone in a hole in some old tree, sound asleep, waiting for night to come so they can go mouse hunting or maybe cutworm hunting.

Dad says screech owls are some of the farmer's best friends, because it's at night that cutworms cause the most trouble, cutting off the little corn shoots and beans and things like that. Since the screech owls hunt them at night, killing hundreds of them, boys ought never to kill any screech owls no matter how much they don't like them.

Poetry was awake too, and pretty soon he whispered, "Bill!"

"What?" I whispered back.

"I've got an idea."

I was still pretty sleepy, so I just grunted.

"Remember Old Man Paddler?" Poetry asked.

That woke me up.

"Yes," I said, and then that screech owl let out another long, trembly wail that sent shivers up and down my spine. When you're home and upstairs in bed listening to an owl out in the woods, it's a whole lot different from when you're sleeping in a tent—which is about the same as sleeping out of doors.

But Poetry didn't pay any attention. He said, "I asked my dad a lot of questions about Old Man Paddler when I got home tonight—without telling him anything—and he said that he was the kindest old man that ever lived and that he especially liked boys!"

I didn't answer, just waiting to see what else Poetry would have to say. I knew he'd thought of something important. I could hear his cot squeaking, as though he was getting up.

"Wait'll I scare that owl away, and I'll tell you," he said.

He fumbled around for his flashlight, turned it on, stepped into his slippers, raised the tent flap, and went out, with me following right behind him—both of us looking like a couple of ghosts in our pajamas. He turned the flashlight up into the tree, and for a moment we saw Mr. Owl with his catlike eyes blinking and looking very fierce and disgusted with us for not appreciating his entertainment. Then he spread his wings and flew like a shadow across the garden toward the barn.

We were standing there in the moonlight after the owl had flown away, when Poetry said so suddenlike that it startled me, "If Old Man Paddler liked boys and was kind to them, and was even a Christian, as Dad says he was, then that wasn't him we saw today! Do you know what I think? I think the man we saw today was wearing a wig and false whiskers. I saw his hands, and they weren't any more an old man's hands than anything. I'll bet he's somebody that's trying to make people think he's Old Man Paddler so he can fool Barry Boyland and get the treasure. And I'll bet Barry knows there's a map and he knows that when his uncle died he left his money somewhere, and Barry's come back to get it."

"But what about the wig and whiskers you found in the tree?" I asked. I couldn't figure out what Poetry was driving at.

"They belonged to the man we saw today. When I found them, he had to get some new ones."

That sounded sensible, and I told Poetry so.

"Also," Poetry said, just like a real detective explaining things, "as long as Barry Boyland is in the hospital, it's up to us boys to protect his interests."

"Maybe we ought to tell the police," I said, thinking what my dad would say we ought to do.

"Not on your life! Think we want to have them spoil our fun?"

Well, I didn't want to argue with Poetry. Besides, his ideas were nearly always right.

We had started to go back into the tent when he stopped so quickly I bumped into him.

"Listen!" he said.

I didn't hear anything, but I did see something that looked like a light in the woods, maybe not far from the sycamore tree.

Maybe I forgot to tell you that old sycamore tree down along the swamp was nearer to Poetry's house than it was to any of the rest of the gang's, being maybe not more than a quarter of a mile away. To get to it from Poetry's house you just had to go down a hill and through the woods.

"Get your binoculars—quick!" Poetry commanded under his breath. He handed me his flashlight, and in a jiffy I was in the tent and out again and Poetry was looking through my binoculars down the hill toward where we knew the tree was.

"Look!" he whispered and handed the binoculars back to me.

All I could see was a light and a shadow moving about it.

"We've got to do something quick!" Poetry said. "We won't even have time to dress." He was in the tent and out again with the disguise he'd found in the old tree day before yesterday.

"What are you going to do?" I asked, my teeth chattering—and not because I was cold either, for it was a warm night. I noticed that Poetry had put on his shoes, so I put mine on too, real fast.

"Let's go, or we'll be too late!" he said.

Now, I didn't exactly want to run smack into any ghosts or whatever was down along the swamp, but I didn't want to seem a coward either. So I followed him as fast as I could. The wind was blowing in our faces, so we knew whoever was there wouldn't hear us coming unless we made a lot of noise.

Poetry looked ridiculous in his big, flapping white pajamas, and I guess I looked just as ridiculous running after him. He knew every inch of the woods along the creek here, so we just hurried along. I still thought his idea was crazy—well, dangerous anyway.

When we got to the bottom of the hill, we stopped to get our breath and to look through the binoculars again. As plain as day, now we could see an old-fashioned lantern and a man digging with a spade right beside the swamp rosebush where we'd been digging that afternoon.

"We'll have to hurry!" Poetry said excitedly. "Look what a big hole he's got already!"

We stooped down low and crawled along as quietly as we could until we were close, so close that if we'd made any noise he'd hear us, and that would spoil everything. Now we could see it was the same old man we'd seen in the afternoon, with the long white hair and the long beard, and he was working terribly fast.

Then I looked at Poetry and guessed what he was going to do, for he was putting on the disguise whiskers and the wig.

"Listen," he whispered in my ear, "you lie flat on the ground right here, and when I let out a long ghost laugh, you turn the flashlight on me quick, and leave it on until I start moaning and talking crazy, and then you turn it off. When I start laughing again, you turn it on again quick!"

Poetry stood up and started waving his arms, and then with that squawky voice of his, which sounded more like a ghost than any real ghost could have sounded, he let out a blood-curdling wail like a screech owl with a bad cold.

I turned the flashlight on him just as he started that wailing. Honest, if I hadn't known who it was, I'd have been scared almost to death. He was swinging his arms, and his pajamas were flapping, and it was enough to scare anybody.

Then Poetry started the most awful moaning you ever heard and saying slowly, *"I . . . am . . . Old . . . Man . . . Paddler's . . . GHOST!"* He yelled the word *ghost* in a deep voice like a man's. Then he let out that terrible laugh and sent the shivers up and down my spine again.

I kept the flashlight turned on him and watched him, waving his white pajamas and looking even worse than a ghost.

Well sir, that man dropped his spade and looked around as if he was scared out of his wits. But in a flash he jumped up and dashed lickety-sizzle straight toward Poetry. Both hands were stretched out in front of him as if he was going to grab Poetry and choke him to death.

And just that second, two shadows darted out from behind some bushes. One of them made a dive for the man's legs in football style, and a voice—it was Big Jim's voice—yelled for us to come and help. I tell you I was glad to hear Big Jim. To tell the truth, I was pretty badly scared and not wanting to let Poetry know it.

It turned out that Big Jim and Circus, who lived right across the road from each other, had decided maybe they'd better stand guard at the rosebush tonight for fear somebody would spoil everything. So they'd hidden in the bushes, having gotten there just a few minutes before we did, coming up the creek from the other direction.

In two shakes of a lamb's tail, all four of us —Big Jim, Circus, Poetry, and I—were scrambling all over the man. His white hair and whiskers came off just as Poetry thought they would, and we saw he had black hair, the same color as the radio had said the bank robber was supposed to have.

The man struck out with his big fists and kicked and swore. One of his fists caught me on the chin and knocked me flat. It didn't hurt much at the time because I was so mad, and things don't seem to hurt so much when you're mad. But I didn't stay down. In a second I was right in the thick of the fight again. I got there just in time to see Poetry's big right foot with his heavy shoe kick the man right on the shin, and the man let out a yell of pain. I was glad right that minute that Poetry had big feet.

I dived in headfirst and got hold of one of the man's legs, and Circus grabbed the other. We held on like a couple of bulldogs or maybe like a pair of snapping turtles holding onto a boy's toes. Pretty soon we had the man down on his stomach, with Poetry lying right across his shoulders and head.

Big Jim knew all the best wrestling tricks and, as I told you before, was terribly strong. Well, he'd gotten that man's arm behind him in what is called the "arm grapevine hold," and that's how it had been so easy for us to get him down and keep him there, in spite of the man's yelling and kicking and swearing and threatening to kill us.

When he was locked up in jail the next day, we learned another reason it had been so easy to keep him down. He had one eye swollen almost shut where Big Jim had hit him with his fist. It took Big Jim's knuckles almost a week to get completely well, he'd hit the man so hard.

Anyway, that's where Little Jim's gunnysack came in handy. We'd left it by the rosebush when we'd been scared away in the afternoon. As I told you, Big Jim knew how to tie twenty-one different kinds of knots. Well, he knew how to make rope too. He took his knife and cut that sack into strips and twisted them together. In almost no time he had that robber's legs and hands tied so that he couldn't get away.

After we got him tied, we didn't know what to do with him.

"What'll we do with him?" Big Jim asked.

"Let's bury him," Circus suggested, not meaning it, of course. "He's got his grave already dug."

That started our prisoner to swearing as I'd never heard any man swear in my life. I was glad Little Jim wasn't there, because he just naturally loved Jesus so much that when anybody used His name like that it made Little Jim feel terribly bad.

The man began to kick and squirm and try to get loose, not knowing that Big Jim was an expert at tying knots.

Then all of a sudden Circus let out a yell and picked up something shiny that had been lying right there on the ground by the man's lantern. At first I could hardly believe my eyes, but there it was in Circus's hand as plain as day—a real honest-to-goodness revolver!

I guess our faces were pretty sober right then, for we realized how serious things were, and how maybe one of us might have been shot.

I didn't tell any of the boys at the time, although I did tell Poetry later, but I just shut my eyes for a moment and whispered a thank-you prayer. "Dear God," I said, "thank You for not letting any of us boys get killed." And I *was* thankful too, I can tell you.

Big Jim took the gun, opened it, and saw that it was loaded. Then he said grimly in a voice that sounded awful fierce, "And now, Mr. Whoever-you-are, I've got your gun pointing right straight toward you! You lie still while we get the sheriff!"

Poetry was delegated to run home for his dad, which he did. His father phoned the sheriff and then came down himself to help us guard the robber until the police got there.

That black-haired man must have thought Poetry was a real ghost, or else that Old Man Paddler had come to life again, or he wouldn't have been so upset. Anyway that's what I was thinking that night while we were going back to Poetry's tent.

We'd gotten to the rosebush just in time

too, I thought, for right down in the hole where the robber had been digging we'd found a rusty steel box, which must have been buried by Old Man Paddler himself.

Of course, as Poetry's dad said while we were all still waiting there in the lantern light for the sheriff to come, taking turns holding that steel box on our laps, "Barry Boyland will have to prove he is really and truly the old man's nephew before his treasure, or whatever it is, will be given to him."

Well, at last Poetry and I were on our cots again with the same stars looking down at us through the opening in the tent and with the same wind sighing through the leaves in the maple overhead. Of course, we weren't going to get to sleep right away, because we were pretty excited and so pleased with ourselves that we didn't know what to do. But then I got sleepier and sleepier, and the next thing I knew, it was morning.

# 10

Maybe I never told you that if it hadn't been for the gang, I'd have been really lonesome. You see, I didn't have any brothers or sisters. And when you're the only child in the house, you keep wishing and wishing you weren't. I guess I wanted a little brother as much as I wanted anything in the world.

Anyway, when I told Poetry good-bye that morning, I couldn't help but think how nice it would be to have just one brother, even if he was littler than I was.

I was still feeling that way when I came up to the back door of our house, carrying my suitcase. Just then Dad came hurrying in from the barn with his teeth shining under his mustache and with the happiest smile on his face you ever saw. First he picked me up in his big strong arms and whirled me around in a circle, crying, "Hurrah! Hurrah! Bill Collins!" as if he was extra happy to see me.

I thought maybe he'd heard about us catching the robber, and I could hardly wait until we got in the house so I could tell him and Mom all about it. But then all of a sudden I heard a baby crying, and something inside of me just kind of bubbled up as it does when I want to tell Jesus I love Him, and I knew that a new baby had come to live with us.

"The grandest surprise for you!" Dad said. "The grandest brand new baby in the world!"

And I could see myself having a little brother to play with and not being so lonesome anymore when I was at home.

"A brother?" I asked, hoping it wasn't a girl. In fact, I'd made up my mind to be mad if it was a girl, because I wanted a brother so badly.

"It's a girl!" Dad said. "The prettiest, blue-eyed, curly-haired little sister a boy ever had given to him!" He was so pleased he couldn't keep still. He picked up my suitcase and said, "Come on, Bill Collins, and see our little Charlotte Ann!"

Now why in the world I didn't like the name *Charlotte Ann* I didn't know. But then, I didn't want a baby sister either. So I hung back, not wanting to go into the house. Besides, I was disappointed because I wanted them to be excited over our catching the robber—supposing, of course, they'd heard about it. But instead, they were making a big fuss over the new baby.

I went into the kitchen but not a step farther.

"Well, Bill Collins!" Dad said, surprised. "Aren't you glad?"

The fact is, I wasn't. I didn't like girls very well, I'll have to admit.

But I guess Dad understands boys, for he didn't make me go in. He just went in himself, and pretty soon I could hear him talking with

Mom about me and also making funny cooing noises to the baby.

"He wanted a little brother," Dad said.

Mom answered something I couldn't hear, and then I heard some other woman talking too.

Just to be sure I wasn't missing anything, I peeped around the corner of the door and saw that the other woman had on a nurse's uniform.

I decided to go outdoors.

Dad had planted some early potatoes in a special garden down along the orchard next to the road, and they were already up and growing. So I went to the toolhouse and got the hoe and started hoeing potatoes without being told to.

I stayed mad all morning and wouldn't go into the house at all. Dad just let me work and work, without saying much of anything to me. He was plowing in the field behind the orchard, and I noticed he was whistling and singing. Every half hour, or even less, he'd tie up the horses at the fence and go to the house. To see the new baby, I was sure. It looked as if I wasn't going to be so important around our home anymore.

About eleven o'clock I began to feel worse and worse. Two or three times I even got mad at myself because tears came into my eyes. I felt so sorry for myself. But then I began to get hungry, and I decided maybe I'd just go in at noon and eat dinner anyway. That is, if they'd have a plate set for me.

Just when I was feeling the worst, Dragonfly

came along, stopped on the other side of the fence, and said, "Hello, Bill!"

"Hello," I said, without looking up. My hoe slipped, and I cut off one of the biggest potatoes in the garden. But I didn't care. I just took the hoe and chopped the potato to pieces and covered it up and went on hoeing, after wiping the sweat off my forehead.

"What's the matter?" Dragonfly asked. "What are you so mad about?"

"Nothing," I said, "except I've got a new baby sister!" I kept on hoeing.

Dragonfly looked kind of glum and didn't say a word for a minute. Then he asked, "How old is she?"

"I don't know," I said.

"I'll bet she's ugly," he said. "Girls always are when they're little."

Now, do you know, I didn't like to hear Dragonfly say that. In fact I resented it. "She's pretty," I said, forgetting that I hadn't even looked at her. "She's got pretty blue eyes and black curls!"

"Yeah, but she's a girl, though."

I was still disgusted and said, "Yeah, that's the trouble."

"But as soon as she's big enough, maybe you won't have to help with the dishes anymore," he said.

That was the first encouraging thing I'd thought of all morning, so I kind of sighed.

Since there was a peach tree right close by with a lot of nice shade under it, Dragonfly and

I lay down in the grass and talked a long time about different things, mostly about last night and Old Man Paddler. Dragonfly was surprised at what had happened, and he felt bad to think he hadn't been there to help us catch the robber. We kept on talking until Dad called me to dinner.

Then Dragonfly got up and hurried home, suddenly remembering his mom had told him not to come over to my house this morning.

It seemed funny for Dad to call me to dinner when all my life I'd been used to having Mom do it, but then I supposed she had to take care of the new baby.

At the table Dad prayed a little longer than usual. He was so happy on account of that baby. Mom wasn't feeling very well, so she didn't come to the table. Besides, she had to look after the baby. The nurse carried a tray in to her and then came back and sat in Mom's place.

It didn't seem right to have another woman sitting there, and I got to thinking maybe right after dinner I'd better go in the other room and see Mom anyway. If the baby was there, I'd just sort of look at it kind of quick without particularly noticing it.

Well, pretty soon dinner was over, and I went over to the corner of the dining room where I always kept my straw hat. Neither Dad nor the nurse paid any attention to me, at least so I could notice. I kept looking at the door to the other room out of the corner of my eye, wanting to go in and pretending to be having trouble with one of the buckles on my overalls suspender.

Then, hardly knowing I was going to, I sidled into the bedroom.

And there was Mom in bed with the happiest smile on her face. Beside her, snuggled close and lying in the crook of her arm was the baby.

I guess I never did feel so bashful in my life. I stood there, holding my straw hat in both hands, looking down at my bare feet.

"Come here a minute," Mom said.

I walked over close to the bed and started looking at some roses in a vase on a table. They were about the color of the goldenrod writing paper we used in school, only the petals were soft like velvet. Dad had sent clear to Australia to get the seed, and he'd grown them himself out in our garden.

Say, those yellow roses had the sweetest perfume! Their color made me think of the bed of wild fawn lilies I'd seen down along the creek only yesterday. I guess the real name for fawn lilies is "dogtooth violet," only Dad says they aren't violets. There *were* some blue and purple violets right close by that bed of fawn lilies, though.

Pretty soon I said to Mom, "Do you think she'd like a bouquet of flowers from down along the creek? Maybe I'll have time to go pick some for her."

"I'm sure she would," Mom said, and her face was happier than ever. Honest, I'd never seen her so happy, and I could tell by the way she looked at me that she didn't like my little sister a bit better than she did me.

In about a minute I was out of doors, climbing over the fence, and running like a deer through the woods, following the little footpath to the spring. I was going to pick the biggest bouquet of flowers anybody ever saw for little Charlotte Ann.

I was stooping down right in the middle of that bed of fawn lilies when I heard somebody coming.

It was Circus. "Hello, Bill!" he said. "What you doin'?"

"Nothing," I said. "I got a new baby sister." And I went on picking flowers, suddenly remembering that Circus didn't like girls very well.

"I thought you wanted a little brother!" he grunted, as if he was disgusted with me for not getting what I wanted.

"She's awful nice," I said. "Black hair and blue eyes and—"

"I've got three sisters," Circus said, "and they've all got blue eyes. There ain't anything special about blue eyes." Just then he saw a good climbing tree, and in two seconds he was halfway up to the first limb.

It made me plumb disgusted the way he talked. *Whatever makes him not like girls, anyway?* I thought.

Pretty soon the whole gang was there except Big Jim, who had to do some work before he could come.

"Bill's got a baby sister!" Circus called down

to the gang from where he was sitting, looking like a chimpanzee there on the first limb of the tree.

"Yeah, and she's got blue eyes and long black curls," Dragonfly said, teasing me.

"He's picking flowers for her," Poetry said.

They all knew how I'd wanted a little brother. *Even Poetry is teasing me*, I thought.

I just kept on picking flowers, getting madder every minute and liking my little sister better than ever.

"I'll help you," Little Jim said. "I'll bet she'll like these." He started to pick some harebells over by the beech tree where all of us boys had carved our initials. It was the kind of tree you could do that on.

Little Jim always did stick up for a fellow when he was getting teased. And in a minute Poetry acted as if he was ashamed for having said anything, so he lay down in the grass and started picking flowers himself, reciting,

> "Buttercups and daisies,
>   Oh, the pretty flowers;
> Coming ere the springtime,
>   To tell of sunny hours;
> While the trees are leafless,
>   While the fields are bare . . ."

Only the trees weren't leafless, and the fields weren't bare.

I finished my bouquet and ran home with it

as fast as I could. Little Jim went with me, because he wanted to see the baby too.

"What's her name?" he asked, panting for breath.

"Charlotte Ann."

"It's a pretty name," he said. "I wish I had a little sister." And right then I decided I liked Little Jim an awful lot, almost as well as Poetry.

When we got back to the gang, Big Jim was there. We all lay around in the grass talking about what had happened last night and explaining to Dragonfly and Little Jim that we couldn't help it that they weren't there to get in on the fun. We all kept looking at Big Jim's sore knuckles and kind of envied him for being able to hit the robber so hard it almost knocked him unconscious.

Then we decided to go look at the sycamore tree and the big hole in the ground. After that, Big Jim said, we'd hike up into the hills to see the cabin where Old Man Paddler used to live.

Pretty soon we were all standing around the hole by the big swamp rosebush and being glad the robber was safe in jail where he couldn't hurt anybody. The grass was mashed down where we'd had our fight.

Little Jim just walked around with a sober face. He seemed to be thinking. Then all of a sudden he said, "I'll bet if I'd been here and had got hold of one of his legs, I wouldn't have let go!"

"He only *had* two legs," Dragonfly said, "and Bill and Circus had both of them."

Little Jim looked disappointed for a moment, then his face lit up. "But I could have helped *sit* on him after you got him down, couldn't I?"

*Of course he could,* I thought, but Dragonfly spoiled it by saying, "Not with Poetry sitting on him too. There wouldn't have been room enough!"

We all lay down in the grass then, and Poetry and I told the whole story all over again, not forgetting to tell how ridiculous Poetry had looked in his big, flapping pajamas and with the long hair and whiskers on.

After that, Big Jim called a meeting and gave us a little talk about crime never paying. He quoted a kind of scary verse from the Bible that says, "Do not be deceived, God is not mocked; for whatever a man sows, this he will also reap." Then he explained that if anybody lived a sinful life, he'd have to suffer for it sometime, not only in this life but in the life after this one. And he made us promise we'd never—any of us—ever steal anything as long as we lived.

When he got through, Little Jim piped up. "One of the Ten Commandments says, 'You shall not steal.'"

When the meeting was over, and we were on our way up into the hills, climbing toward Old Man Paddler's cabin, I felt as if we'd all been to church.

I kept thinking as we walked along about that beautiful sunset I'd seen night before last. The sun had been shining through long, pinkish clouds, looking like a waterfall tumbling over a dam with colored electric lights behind it. And I remembered how, pretty soon, those clouds had changed so that they looked like the bars of a jail.

One cloud had looked like an old man with long whiskers. I kept thinking about Old Man Paddler and wondering what he was doing up in heaven—if he was there. And he was if he was dead, because Little Jim said that if people let Jesus into their hearts while they are alive, He'd let them into heaven when they died. Of course, my folks had taught me that too, a long time ago, but Little Jim's saying it reminded me it was true.

We had a lot of fun climbing up to the old cabin. We pretended that Big Jim was the sheriff and the rest of us were his posse and we were going up to ambush a band of robbers who lived there.

In about a half hour, I reckon, we were close enough to the cabin to see it. So we all stopped and lay down in the grass and made plans as to how we'd capture those imaginary robbers.

It made me feel creepy to remember that some people believed the old house was haunted. We knew that was because Old Man Paddler had just disappeared without anybody knowing what had become of him. Everybody finally decided he'd either drowned in the creek or else wandered too far off the path out into the dangerous part of the swamp and had sunk into the quicksand.

Well, we made our plans and sneaked around from tree to tree and from bush to bush until we were real close to the cabin.

All of a sudden Dragonfly said, "Psst!" and we knew he'd either heard or seen something.

We all stopped dead in our tracks and listened, and I guess my red hair must have stood right up on end. I think we all heard it at once —a sort of low moan, as if somebody was trying to call for help and couldn't because his mouth was covered with a blanket or something.

# 11

I closed my teeth together tight to keep them from chattering, because I didn't want anybody to know how scared I was.

I noticed Big Jim look around quick to see if Little Jim was there and all right. It was grand the way he looked after that little fellow. He couldn't have liked him any better if they'd been brothers, I thought. And I made up my mind that even if Charlotte Ann wasn't a boy, I was going to like her just as much as Big Jim liked Little Jim, and I'd protect her and take care of her too. Thinking that made me so I wasn't nearly as afraid as I had been just a half a minute before.

I could see Big Jim was making up his mind to do something, for we could still hear that muffled voice in the cabin, maybe calling for help. I kept thinking, *What if whoever is in there is just trying to get us to come in so he can catch us in a trap!* But we couldn't afford to lie there waiting if somebody was really needing us.

So pretty soon Big Jim told us to keep still while he and Circus went to investigate.

In just about a minute we saw Circus standing in the doorway of the old cabin and motioning for us to come quick. I tell you, it didn't take us long to scramble to our feet and get there.

What do you think we saw the minute we got in? It looked as if there were only two rooms in the cabin, and on a cot in the corner of the first one was an old man with long white hair and whiskers and his hands and feet tied with strips of blanket. Big Jim was just taking a gag out of his mouth, which somebody had put there to keep him from calling for help, I suppose. He looked exactly like the picture I'd seen of Old Man Paddler, the picture Barry Boyland had given my dad in the hospital yesterday morning. He also looked like the robber we'd caught last night before his wig and beard had come off.

"Water!" the old man cried in a broken voice.

I thought of the map we'd found and of the picture of an old man in bed, asking a nurse for more water.

Dragonfly looked around quick and found an old tin can on a table. Then he and I ran out and down the hill to where we'd seen a spring on our way up.

"I wonder who he is," Dragonfly said, panting for breath.

"Old Man Paddler, of course," I said.

"But how can he be? He's dead!"

"He doesn't look like it, does he?"

"He's supposed to be, anyway," Dragonfly said.

In about two minutes we were back with the water, and the old man drank as if he hadn't had any for a long time. We were careful not to let him drink too much or too fast, because it might not be good for him.

Pretty soon he was sitting up in bed and thanking us boys for coming to his rescue. He'd been tied up here since yesterday, he said, and he hadn't had a drink since last night. He had the kindest little gray eyes, and you could tell by the way he looked at us that he liked boys. And that's how we decided he must be the real Old Man Paddler.

"You *aren't* a ghost, are you?" Little Jim asked. You could see he liked the old man an awful lot. Little Jim always did like old people and was kind to them.

That old man just laughed right out loud when Little Jim said that. He told us he'd left the hills about ten years ago and had traveled around the world, visiting many countries. He said he had decided to come back home and live the rest of his life here in the hills. . . .

But suddenly he stopped telling us about himself and looked around as if he were afraid. And that gave us the idea we ought to tell him about the robber being caught and his nephew getting shot and how his treasure was locked up in the big vault in the bank uptown right this minute—if it was really his treasure. So we told him, all of us helping a little bit.

You should have seen the worried look leave his face. All of a sudden he said, "I bet you boys are hungry."

We weren't. That is, we'd rather have heard his side of the story first—how he happened to get tied up and anything else he wanted to tell us.

"I'll bet *you're* hungry," Circus said.

We began looking around to see if there was anything to eat.

That robber we'd caught must have been living in Old Man Paddler's cabin for quite a while. He had laid in a supply of food—canned pork and beans and corn and all kinds of fruits. And Old Man Paddler himself had brought some when he'd come home yesterday afternoon.

We carried in wood and built a fire in the old stove and carried in a kettle of water for him.

"I dug some sassafras roots yesterday on the way home," he said, looking in a can on an old shelf. "How'd you boys like to have some tea? It's very good for boys."

Sassafras tea, you know, is made from the sweet-smelling roots of the sassafras tree. The roots are a reddish color, and you cut them in little chunks and boil them in water till the water turns red. With sugar in it, it beats any other kind of tea all to pieces for taste. Anyway, I think so. Little Jim had never tasted any before, and he said it was just like drinking lollipop juice.

I don't suppose I can tell Old Man Paddler's story as he told it, and maybe it'll sound more like me telling it than him. But I'll do the best I can because it's a real story.

As I said, as soon as he heard about the robber being caught and put in jail, he didn't act worried or afraid anymore. So now he had us sit down and listen. Big Jim sat on a chair with Little Jim on the cot beside him, and the rest of us sprawled on the floor. The old man sat in the only other chair in the cabin, one he himself had made out of hickory years ago. Sitting there, he looked just like one of the pictures of Moses I'd seen in my Bible storybook at home, my parents having bought me one with a lot of pictures in it when I was little.

Old Man Paddler had been traveling around the world, visiting a lot of countries, staying maybe a month or two in each place. He was rich, you know. Then he got to thinking maybe he was too old to travel anymore, and if he died he ought to do something with all the money he'd buried back on the hill beside the swamp.

I guess if you'd seen us boys while he was telling us that story—with his kind old eyes looking at us as if we were his very own grand-children, his long whiskers bobbing every time his chin moved—you'd have thought we all should have been named Dragonfly. That was the most exciting story we'd ever heard, and our eyes were almost popping out of our heads —anyway, they were wide open every minute of the story.

"When I got back here from my trip around the world," Old Man Paddler said, "I was so tired I didn't feel very well. So I stopped down there by my spring to get a drink and rest, won-dering if anything had happened to my cabin while I was away. I hadn't intended to stay so long when I left, you know. Then I looked up and saw smoke coming out of the chimney!

"*Who's in my cabin?* I thought. I hurried up the hill and pushed open the door. There sitting at my table and drinking coffee was a man who looked almost exactly like me. It was just like looking at my twin, or else in a mirror, and I began to wonder if maybe I was losing my mind, being so old.

"'Who are you?' I asked.

"And the strange man just laughed and said, 'I'm Old Man Paddler, of course. What do you want?' and he swore at me.

"Well, right away I knew I hadn't lost my mind, and that the man *wasn't* me, because I don't swear. Haven't since I was a little boy and let Jesus Christ come into my heart.

"'You can't swear in my house!' I told him.

"Well, that man stood up and glared at me," Old Man Paddler said, "and then all of a sudden he grabbed me and pulled me inside and pointed a gun at me and shouted, 'I *am* Old Man Paddler! Do you hear? And you're just a visitor! Come here! I'm going to cut your whiskers off!'

"I'm not very strong anymore, and I couldn't have done anything to protect myself, so all I could do was beg him not to. Anyway, he seemed to change his mind and said he guessed he'd kill me instead and throw me into the swamp. 'Everybody thinks you're dead anyway, and we'd just as well let it be true!' he said.

"First he tied me up and threw me on the bed. Then he got a mirror and came over to where I was and began looking into it. He'd look first at me, then into the mirror.

"'I look exactly like you,' he said. 'I'm certainly glad you came home so I know exactly how I'm supposed to look.'

"I had to admit he did look just like me. I kept lying there, wishing my nephew would come. You see, about a week before I came home, I'd sent a letter to my only living relative out in California, telling him to please come to see me, as I was getting old and had a lot of money to give him before I died. In that letter I told him where he would find a map that would explain where I'd buried my money, so in case anything happened to me before he got here he'd know where to find it. I explained the map too, just in case he wouldn't be able to figure out what the different things meant."

The old man stopped a moment, and we all sighed, waiting eagerly for him to finish. That map, we knew, was the one we'd found in the old sycamore tree day before yesterday.

"Well," the old man went on, while I shifted my feet to a more comfortable position, one of them having gone to sleep because I was sitting on it, "my twin stood there glaring at me, trying to decide what he'd better do with me. I tell you, boys, I'm an old man, and I thought maybe my time had come to die. So I just shut my eyes and started praying and telling the Father in heaven I was ready if He wanted me.

"But then I remembered again all that money I'd buried and was going to give my nephew, and maybe he wouldn't even get my letter, and the money would be wasted. In my travels around the world, I'd seen so many places where missionaries were needed, and I thought that maybe in a few minutes I'd be in heaven seeing Jesus face-to-face and He'd ask me why I hadn't used some of that money for missionary work . . ."

Then the old man went on with his story. "The robber heard me praying, and it made him angry. 'Shut up!' he shouted and raised his fist like he was going to hit me. So I did stop praying out loud, although I kept right on praying silently, knowing God could hear anyway, and telling Him I was ready to die because I knew He'd sent His Son, Jesus, to save me, and I had believed on Him in my heart.

"'All right, Grandpa!' the fierce-looking man said roughly. 'Let's get those whiskers off! Or shall I take you out somewhere and bury you?' He came over to me and took hold of my beard and gave it a little jerk. Then he laughed and said, 'They're real whiskers all right, and your hair is genuine too. I lost a wig and beard just like the ones I have on now down by the swamp a few days ago.'

"He stood there looking at me as if he was trying to think of some way to get mine off so he could use them himself in case he needed them. I could see he was a wicked man and might do anything. And with his gun pointing straight at me, I began to think how I might save my life for a little while at least, so I said, 'Maybe you'd like to know where my money is buried.'"

The old man poured himself another cup of sassafras tea. "All the time I was hoping my nephew would come, yet afraid to have him come because he might get hurt. So I told the robber where to dig, and he must have decided to let me live a little while longer, for he put a gag in my mouth and went away, leaving me all tied up like you found me. Just as he went out the door, he said, 'Listen, Grandpa Paddler, if you've lied to me, I'll come back! And you can tell this world good-bye!' And that was the last I saw of him."

The old man sighed as if he was tired of talking.

Anyway, that was his side of the story, and you know what happened after that—how the robber had seen us boys digging there by the rosebush and that night had come back himself and we had captured him.

We thanked Old Man Paddler for telling us the story and promised to come back and see him again and that we'd go see his nephew and tell him his uncle was alive and well and not to worry. He thanked us over and over again for coming to untie him, and then we left.

Down by the spring where Dragonfly and I had gone for water, we all lay down one at a time and drank, horse fashion. Then we looked back up at the cabin. Blue smoke was rising slowly out of the chimney, and the old man was standing in the doorway, his long white whiskers shining in the afternoon sun.

He lifted his hand and waved good-bye to us—no, he had both hands raised, like in the pictures in my Bible storybook where an old prophet was raising his hands to bless somebody. For a minute I thought of the funny cloud I'd seen the other night, which had looked like an old man with long gold whiskers reaching down to his waist.

Then we started down the hill toward home, not forgetting to stop at the swimming hole for a good swim so we could tell our folks we wouldn't need a bath tonight, this being Saturday and all boys having to take a bath on Saturday night whether they want to or not.

Some of us had to take them even oftener than that.

# 12

Did I tell you that we nearly always went to town on Saturday nights? We had to, you know, to buy groceries and things. So when we were dressed, Dad called and soon we were driving along in our car toward town, which was about five miles away.

"Now, don't you get into any mischief!" Dad said to me when we stopped in front of the big fountain on the main street.

I slid out of the car and ran over to where Poetry and Dragonfly were waiting for me.

"Hello, Bill," they said.

"Hello, Dragonfly. Hello, Poetry." They were both wearing their Sunday clothes.

We stood watching the water spraying down from above and falling into a big cement pool right in front of us. Electric lights shone down on it from lampposts all around. You could see maybe a dozen goldfish swimming around in the pool.

With the water splashing and the band playing up the street and hundreds of people standing around talking and laughing, and especially with Poetry and Dragonfly there, all of us liking each other a lot, it seemed good to be alive.

"I wonder if it's deep enough to swim in," Poetry said.

I was thinking the same thing, and probably so was Dragonfly. And do you know we had to go away and quit watching that fountain because it made us want to go swimming so bad it made us feel sad all over! We started walking along Main Street, Poetry in the middle and Dragonfly and me on each side of him.

All of a sudden Dragonfly said, "Psst!" just as he always does when he's seen or heard something important.

So we stopped quick to find out what it was.

"It's Circus's dad!" he said. "See him walking crazylike? I bet he's drunk again!"

And sure enough, he was.

"I hope he hasn't got a gun," I said, remembering that he always carried one when he went hunting, and he was an awful good shot.

He kept shuffling along, reaching out with each foot as though he was having trouble finding the sidewalk.

"Let's follow him to see where he goes," Poetry said.

Pretty soon he staggered up to a place where they sell beer and kind of fell against the door. Then he pushed it open and went inside.

We stood looking in through the smoky-glass door panel and saw him lean up against the bar, throw down some money, and say something to the bartender. It was disgusting to see the big, fat-stomached bartender take the money and give him another glass of beer, when I knew Circus's folks were poor and needed all the money they could get for food and clothes and things.

I was glad Little Jim wasn't with us. He would have felt bad about it. He liked Circus so well that he wouldn't have had any fun at all. As it was, it sort of took away the good taste of the bag of peanuts we were eating right that minute.

We went on walking around, feeling kind of sad. Pretty soon we saw Circus himself sitting alone on a bench in front of an empty store building, looking like he'd lost his best friend.

"Hello, Circus," I said, and Poetry and Dragonfly said the same thing. We offered him some of our peanuts and sat down beside him.

"What's the matter?" I asked.

But he didn't answer. He just kept sitting there, looking unhappy, not even taking any peanuts. I noticed he didn't have on nearly as nice clothes as the rest of us, though they were clean and neat. His shoes were old too, but he had them pretty well polished, and they looked all right. He had a very good mother.

"Wait a minute," Dragonfly said. He got up and ran down the street and came back with a big bag of fresh popcorn, knowing Circus liked popcorn better than anything.

But Circus didn't even take any popcorn, and we didn't try very hard to make him. We all sat there feeling unhappy, none of us saying anything for a long time.

And finally Circus said, "Dad's drunk again." Then he sighed and took some of my peanuts and Dragonfly's popcorn.

Up the street, the band was playing a beautiful number, "The Stars and Stripes Forever." People were walking past in front of us, going both ways, talking and laughing. Everybody seemed happy except us.

"That's a pretty band piece," Circus said. "I always wanted to play in a band. Maybe someday I'll run away from home and get a job and make enough money to buy a cornet."

"Doesn't your mother like you anymore?" Dragonfly asked.

Circus choked on the popcorn he had in his mouth and coughed a little. Then he said, "Maybe if I ran away and got some work, I could send her the money I made."

Just then Circus's dad came shuffling down the street.

In an instant, Circus was out of his seat and running into an alley as fast as he could go with us right after him. I thought maybe he was going to run away from home right now, and I didn't want him to because I knew how his mother would feel.

In the alley about a block from the main street, we stopped behind somebody's garage, where there wasn't any light, and listened for a minute to see if anybody was coming. Nobody was.

"He's mad at me," Circus said, "'cause I went into the saloon about a half hour ago and told him to stop drinking or I'll tell Mother. He'll give me a terrible lickin' if he catches me."

Right beside us was a telephone pole, and I

couldn't help but think that, if Circus was happy, he'd likely be halfway to the top of it by now. There was also the brightest, roundest moon up in the sky, and if Poetry had been happy, he'd probably have started to say:

"Hey, diddle, diddle,
    The cat and the fiddle,
 The cow jumped over the moon;
    The little dog laughed to see such sport,
    And the dish ran away with the spoon."

We stayed there in the shadow of that little garage for maybe five minutes, thinking and saying different things.

I was wishing Circus was my brother so he could have my dad for his daddy when all of a sudden we heard footsteps coming down the alley. We crowded down behind a big box and waited. And would you believe it? In a minute two men stopped there in the dark, and one of them was my dad and the other was Circus's. You can guess we had a hard time keeping still, and I can't tell you how weird I felt inside.

"You're making a big fool out of yourself!" my dad said disgustedly.

Circus's dad swore and said, "I don't want any more kids! Three girls and one good-for-nothing boy is enough!"

My fists doubled up when he said that. I knew he was talking about Circus, and I reckon maybe it isn't wrong to get mad at something like that.

I peeped out from behind the box, and I could see my dad standing there tall and straight in the moonlight, looking clean and good. Circus's dad was slouched over with his hat on crooked and some of his mussed-up hair sticking out on one side. His tie was twisted, and his face, what I could see of it, looked terrible.

For a minute I remembered what Big Jim had said that afternoon about sin, quoting from the Bible, "Do not be deceived, God is not mocked!" I decided nobody could fool God. It was like my dad had just said—Circus's father was making a big fool out of himself.

"Now you listen, Dan Browne!" my dad said roughly. "You're not drinking another drop tonight, do you hear?"

"'S'none of your business!" Circus's father grumbled back and swore again. "It's my money, and I'll spend it like I please. Anyway, when a new baby comes to my house, I've got a right to celebrate."

But now my dad was getting angry—with the right kind of anger. He just reached out his big strong hands, grabbed Circus's dad by the shoulders, shook him the way a big dog shakes a rat, and said, "You ought to celebrate by getting down on your knees, Dan Browne, and praying to God Almighty that He'll forgive your sins and make you a good father to your children and a decent husband to your wife. Mrs. Browne is one of the grandest little women that ever drew breath, and your boy is one of the finest boys in the county. And you—shame on you, Dan Browne!"

Well, my dad wouldn't let Circus's father go home that night, because he knew he'd make all kinds of trouble and maybe do something terrible. So he hunted up the town marshal, which is the same as a policeman, and they locked him up in jail, which is where he belonged.

And that's how we came to learn that Circus had a new baby at his house too. Also, that's how Circus came to stay all night at my house. With the new baby at his place, there might be a lot of excitement. Besides, Big Jim's mother was staying there, too, to help take care of the baby, so there wouldn't be enough beds. Circus said he would just as soon sleep in the barn—he'd done it before when his dad was mad at him about something.

But they wouldn't want a noisy boy around right now, so my dad drove all the way to Circus's house to tell them that Circus was going to sleep with me that night, his folks not having a telephone because his dad used most all their money for whiskey and beer. Then Dad stopped at Big Jim's house and made arrangements for somebody to do the chores at Circus's the next morning, since Big Jim lived right across the road from them anyway.

# 13

When we got back to our house, it was after ten o'clock, more than an hour past the time I usually went to bed in the summer.

Charlotte Ann was wide awake when we came in and was making a terrible noise. Circus and I went in for a minute to see what all the fuss was about. Miss Trillium, the nurse, was holding her, and that little thing stopped crying the minute we came in. Or, I should have said, the minute she saw Circus!

"I know how to look at girls," he said to me, grinning. "I've got three sisters."

"Four," I said. "You've got a new one at your house."

And he said, "Yeah, that's right," sort of disappointed sounding.

"Good night," I called to Mom in the other room, after watching Charlotte Ann drink her milk for a while. She was the cutest little thing! Even Circus looked at her as if he thought so too, and I got to thinking that maybe he liked his sisters better than he let on. Most boys don't want to let anybody know they like girls at all, even when they do.

Then I looked at Miss Trillium, with her pretty crimson cheeks and blue eyes, and said good night again, special. She was holding a bottle with a nipple on it for Charlotte Ann, and she looked up and smiled at me and said, "Good night, Bill."

Circus said good night too, and she gave him a nice smile but not nearly as nice as the one she'd given me, I thought.

Then Circus and I went upstairs.

Circus didn't seem very happy, and you couldn't blame him with his dad drunk and in jail. But in spite of that, he felt sorry for his dad.

"He's good to us sometimes," he said while we were undressing. "One day last week he told Mom he'd never get drunk again in his life, and I saw him give her a big hug like he really meant it. And Mom cried 'cause she was so happy. But those old newspapers and magazines Dad reads have great big whiskey advertisements in them with important-looking men drinking and saying how good it is. And the first thing you know, Dad goes to town and buys some again."

Then he said, "You know what I wish?"— and I could see he was getting mad at the people who made whiskey and sold it and advertised it. "I wish," he said with his fists doubled up and his voice trembly, "I wish they'd just *once* take a picture of my dad when he's drunk and looking like he did uptown tonight and put *that* in their papers and magazines! I bet *that* wouldn't make anybody want to buy any!"

Circus kept his fists doubled up and looked so fierce it almost scared me. Still, I was kind of proud of him that he could get mad at something like that, because it's all right to get angry at sin. My dad says so. And once even Jesus was angry at some people in the Bible who were doing wrong. I guess maybe God hates sin terribly!

It didn't take us long to get ready for bed, and pretty soon we were under the covers with the lamp out and the moonlight shining in on us. Then I remembered. I hadn't said my prayers.

In fact, I'd been thinking about it quite a while and didn't know what to do. I was sure Circus had never said a prayer in his life because even if he did have a good mother, she wasn't a Christian yet. And she'd never taught him to pray.

So I began to think that maybe I'd say my prayers in bed. But I remembered the story we'd read in school when we were in the fourth grade about "Little Arthur's Prayer" and how that brave little fellow had knelt down before a whole roomful of boys and prayed before going to bed. So I lay thinking, wondering if Circus would make fun of me. Then I began to wonder what Little Jim would do if he were here, and I knew that he wouldn't even think about being afraid or ashamed of praying.

So I decided on something. And talk about being brave in a fight!—I guess I never had any harder time in my life being brave than right that minute. My heart started beating fast, and I was actually scared to do what I knew I had to do.

I asked Circus if he remembered "Little

Arthur's Prayer," and he did. Then I told him about Poetry praying every night before he went to bed. I knew he liked Poetry a lot, so pretty soon I said suddenly, with my heart still beating fast, "Let's us do it too," not telling him I always prayed every night anyway, although I guess maybe I should have.

Circus grunted and then said, "You do it first."

Well, in a twinkle I was out of bed and saying my prayers quietly, as I did sometimes anyway, knowing Jesus could hear me even if I didn't talk out loud. I prayed for Circus's dad there in jail and for his mother and for his new baby sister. Then I jumped up off my knees with my heart as light as a feather and said, "I guess I feel better now." And I climbed into bed over on the other side of Circus.

Circus lay still for about a half minute, and then suddenly there he was down on his knees right where I'd been, his brown hair shining in the moonlight. I guess I never did tell you Circus had the nicest brown hair.

He told me later that he'd never prayed before in his whole life. (I'd never thought about him maybe not knowing what to say.) But then he jumped up real quicklike and said the same thing I'd said when I got up—"I guess I feel better now." He got into bed with his face turned the other way on his pillow.

After a while I said to Circus, "I prayed for your dad."

He didn't say anything.

I wouldn't have found out how terribly bad he felt about his dad if I hadn't put a hand on his shoulder and then felt a teeny wet spot on his pillow like maybe a tear had dropped there.

But I didn't tell him I'd felt it. I just rolled over and said, "Good night."

# 14

When Circus and I woke up the next morning, the sun was already shining into our window, making a big yellow square on the green wallpaper just above the foot of the bed.

We lay there for a minute before getting up, and I was looking at the sunlight when all of a sudden there was a little shadow moving around in it. I knew right away that it was a bird sitting on our windowsill, a sparrow maybe, preening his feathers and making bird noises. His little head with its tiny sharp bill kept bobbing around, just like the bobber on my fishing line had done that day when I'd caught the black bass.

Circus let out a big loud yawn that scared the bird, and it flew away. And just that minute Charlotte Ann started crying downstairs.

"See there!" I said to him, sitting up in bed and pretending to be angry. "You woke her up!"

But he just grinned at me and said, "I'll run downstairs and let her look at me, and she'll stop crying right away." He rolled out of bed.

Both of us dressed in two jiffies, me putting on overalls so I could help Dad with the chores —that is, if they weren't already done.

Then we went tumbling downstairs and out

of doors, like two frisky colts. Just that minute Circus saw our big, high grape arbor with a crosspiece at the top. Right there where there weren't any vines was a good place to do athletic stunts. Quick as a monkey he was right up on it, "skinning the cat" and hanging by his legs.

"Hey!" I cried to him, "you'll get your good clothes all wrinkled and dirty!"

He looked at me surprisedlike, his face looking awful funny upside down, for he was still hanging by his legs. His brown hair was all tangled on top of his head.

He got down right quick and said, "That's right! I have to be careful!" And he really meant it.

But we had so many things for a boy to climb on—such as the big cherry tree, the high rope swing in our walnut tree, and the ladder leading up into the haymow in the barn—that I had to take Circus back upstairs to my room and get a pair of overalls for him, or his clothes wouldn't have been fit to wear to Sunday school. You see, I'd made up my mind he was going to Sunday school with me.

"I *won't* go to Sunday school with you," he said. "My clothes aren't good enough for that." And he looked sort of sad again. Maybe he'd happened to think about his dad in jail. I don't know, but he didn't act like Circus after that, and I felt very sorry for him.

"Besides," he said, "people will look at me and won't like me 'cause my dad's in jail. Anyway, I haven't been to Sunday school since I was little."

Just then my dad came out of the barn with two big pails of milk, each one with about an inch of rich, yellow foam on top.

"Why didn't you wake me up?" I said to him, feeling guilty because I hadn't helped him. Even if I didn't like to work, I do like to help my dad get the work done. It's only good-for-nothing boys that won't help their parents without being scolded.

But Dad just laughed. "You don't have company every day, so I decided to let you sleep."

I thought that was pretty nice of him.

After breakfast Circus and I helped with the dishes. Soon it would be time to go to Sunday school, and he still hadn't made up his mind to go. We all told him his clothes looked good enough, and just to keep him from feeling embarrassed, I put on my second-best shoes instead of my best. And since he didn't have a good cap, we would both go bareheaded.

"Besides," I told him, "I'll bet Jesus didn't have a lot of fancy clothes to wear when He was a little boy 'cause His folks were poor."

"Were they?" he asked, surprised.

"Sure," I said, "and when He grew up, He didn't even have a nice home to live in or any money to pay taxes with. Why, one time He sent Peter down to the lake with his fishing pole and told him he'd find the money to pay their taxes right in the fish's mouth." I explained that Jesus was probably trying to teach Peter that God was able to take care of him.

But Circus, not having heard the Bible explained very much, didn't quite understand what I was talking about.

"Is *that* in the Bible?" he asked.

We were standing up in our big high swing just then, facing each other and pumping ourselves higher and higher.

"Sure it is!" I said. "There's some of the best stories in the world right in the Bible."

"Do you suppose there'll be any jails in heaven?" he asked after a bit.

We were swinging awful high right then, back and forth, the cool air blowing against our faces, our shirt sleeves flapping, our hair getting all mussed up and needing combing again before we could go to church. "Jails!" I said, trying to remember something I'd heard our minister say. "No, I don't think so. What would God want jails up there for!"

Circus didn't say anything for a minute. Then he asked, "Then what'll He *do* with people that get drunk and kill people and things like that?"

"I don't know," I said, thinking I'd ask my dad or mom or Little Jim or somebody as soon as I got a chance. Then I happened to remember. "One day Little Jim said, 'I think maybe all the people who aren't saved won't get into heaven at all but will have to go to . . . to some terrible *jail!*' " I told Circus.

He looked awful sad, and we both forgot to

pump, and our swing started to slow down. "You mean . . . hell?" he asked.

And that's how I began to wonder whether I was saved myself or not. I knew I wasn't a drunk like Circus's dad or a robber like the man at Old Man Paddler's cabin, but I felt that I needed Jesus anyway. For if people didn't *need* Him, why did He come down here from heaven to die for them?

I didn't tell Circus how I felt just then nor my dad nor anybody. But I thought maybe sometime I'd tell Little Jim, and I might even tell Jesus Himself the next time I prayed.

Pretty soon, away we went in Dad's car to Sunday school, stopping at Poetry's house for him and at Dragonfly's for him. Big Jim and Little Jim were waiting for us in front of the church when we got there.

Our class had the nicest teacher. She knew all about boys, and we could tell by the way she looked at us that she liked us and wouldn't get angry if we forgot to listen for a minute or maybe whispered or something. It was especially hard for Poetry to be good in either church or school on account of his being so mischievous. But even a mischievous boy can be good if he wants to.

The only thing wrong with going to Sunday school on a hot day is that you have to wear shoes, and you keep wanting to take them off and go running lickety-sizzle through the woods or go swimming or fishing. And if your teacher doesn't understand boys, it's even harder.

Right after Sunday school, we all went outdoors a while for some fresh air before the bell rang for church to begin. Then we went back inside. Every one of us stayed for church too. Big Jim had talked to us about that once.

You see, for a while last year, after there'd been a fire in our own church, we all went to a Sunday school in town. Right after Sunday school was over, almost half the other boys and girls went home, not even staying for church! Big Jim was disgusted, and Little Jim thought it was terrible. Think of it. Not staying for church service. Shucks! Didn't those kids' parents know *anything?* Didn't they know that if you don't want a boy to grow up to be no good at all, he's got to go to Sunday school and church when he's little! Anybody ought to know *that!*

When we were back inside, my dad saw us boys sitting in a row all by ourselves, with Poetry and me side by side. He gave me a look with his eyebrows down that said, "Now, then, William Jasper Collins! You see to it that you don't get into mischief!"

Maybe our pastor wasn't the most wonderful speaker in the world, and maybe I couldn't understand everything he said, but he always had *something* in his sermon that a boy could understand. And that made it interesting. I guess he remembered when he was a boy and couldn't understand everything either unless it was explained in boy language. Anyway, his sermons helped you to love Jesus a little more. And when he told an interesting story to explain some Bible verse, I always sat up and listened even if I had been wiggling around a little bit before that.

The music started, and we were all singing away. Poetry growled along trying to sing bass, but he couldn't because his voice was half soprano and half something else. Somebody's baby started to cry, and I forgot all about the song and everything else for thinking of Charlotte Ann.

I looked at Circus, and he looked at me. And then he looked at the baby, just as he had looked at Charlotte Ann last night, but it didn't do a bit of good. In fact, the baby cried even louder than before! And for a minute I had a hard time to keep from laughing. But pretty soon they took the baby out.

We finished the song and were starting another when all of a sudden the door opened, and somebody came in and started walking down the aisle toward the front of the church. And would you believe it? It was Old Man Paddler himself, his long white hair combed nice and neat. He had a good suit of clothes on, and he was walking pretty spryly for such an old man, looking just like Moses or somebody.

I tell you, we all sat up and took notice, and for a minute the singing almost stopped. Little Jim's mother, who was playing the piano, turned halfway around and actually struck some of the wrong keys.

Our minister must have known him, for, after looking surprised, he came right down off the platform and went to him and shook hands, smiling all over as though Mr. Paddler was his very best friend. He whispered something in the old man's ear, and I saw the old head nod as though he was saying yes.

Then we went on singing.

Pretty soon I knew what our minister had said to him, for when we'd finished the song and we'd read some verses out of the Bible, he said, "I'm sure we are happy to have one of our charter members with us this morning after a trip around the world, one whom many of you have known and loved. At this time we shall be led in prayer by Seneth Paddler."

And the old man just lifted his fine old gray head toward the ceiling with his face turned up and his eyes shut. And his kind voice started in praying, trembling along as if it wasn't very strong and might break at any time.

I shut my eyes the way you're supposed to when anybody prays, and for a minute it was almost scary in that church because it seemed heaven had moved right down to earth. I actually had to open my eyes to be sure it wasn't so. And, say, that old man's white forehead was shining, and his long whiskers looked awful pretty. I actually kept my eyes open almost all the rest of the way through his prayer, forgetting to close them.

And do you know what? I never told anybody before, but just as Old Man Paddler was finishing his prayer, I shut my eyes real quick and told Jesus I loved Him and asked Him to come into my heart for sure, so I'd know whether I was saved or not. Then I prayed real quick for Circus's dad, too, and got done at the same time Old Man Paddler did.

And do you know what else? From that minute on it seemed that Jesus and I had a secret together. I knew I was a Christian, and I was sure that some day Circus's dad would be saved and wouldn't get drunk anymore, and Circus wouldn't have to run away, for his dad would be good to him, and Circus could have a cornet and play in the band, and his mother would be happy, and they'd all go to church like families are supposed to.

The meeting was over, and we went home, Circus riding with Big Jim and his folks.

After dinner at our house, I saw Dad get his big black Bible and go out to the car. I knew he was going to town to the jail and talk to Circus's dad. So I ran down to the barn and climbed up into our haymow and went way back up in the hay where nobody could see me, or even hear me, and got down on both of my knees and told Jesus about our secret. I asked Him to help Dad and to make that part of the secret about Circus's father come true just as quick as He could.

Then, to make it seem like a bargain, I took my little New Testament—I still had it in my pocket from carrying it to Sunday school—and stuck it there in a crack in a log and left it. And all of a sudden I began to be awful happy because now I was sure that Jesus had truly forgiven my sins. I even cried a little bit all by myself, and I didn't care if I did. I loved Jesus so much inside that it seemed my heart would burst.

When I climbed down out of the haymow, there at the bottom of the ladder was old Mixy, our black-and-white cat. I felt so good I just scooped her up in my arms and hugged her and yelled, "Whoopee!"

But Mixy didn't seem to appreciate the fact that I was happy, for she got scared when I yelled, "Whoopee!" She scrambled out of my arms and went lickety-split across the barn floor and crawled into a hole that leads under the barn.

Then I went up to the house to see Charlotte Ann and maybe do a little errand or something for Miss Trillium, if she wanted me to, and to wait for Dragonfly, who had promised to come over to play with me that afternoon.

# 15

Charlotte Ann still wasn't very cheerful, nothing like I hoped she would be a week or two later when she'd gotten used to living in this world and maybe had decided that my red hair and freckles weren't anything to be afraid of.

She didn't need to act so disgusted with my hair! When you got a look at her black curls up real close, they looked as if maybe they'd be dark red themselves some day. But then, of course, she didn't know that. Babies don't know anything, in fact; *nearly* all babies don't, except Charlotte Ann.

I stood there beside Mom's bed, where she was resting, and I looked at the golden fawn lilies I'd picked, with the blue and purple violets mixed up with them.

"Do you think she liked them?" I asked Mom.

I was getting awful lonesome for my mom. And I tell you, it wasn't going to be easy to let Charlotte Ann have all the attention around the house. My dad was just crazy about that little thing! Watching him, if you didn't happen to notice how big he was or see his mustache, you couldn't tell him from Circus, for he'd almost stand on his head in front of Charlotte Ann just to get her to smile at him. And he'd make the funniest faces! It was almost disgusting to see him make over her like that. That is, it was until one day I caught myself doing the same thing, and then it didn't seem so bad. But that's getting pretty far ahead of my story, because little Charlotte Ann didn't even know enough to smile until she was several weeks old.

I kept waiting for Dragonfly to come, wondering why he was so late. But finally I saw him running up the road just as fast as he could. He opened our gate quick and hurried up to the house. I ran out to meet him.

After taking a long walk, we had a drink at the spring, and then we took turns looking at different things with my binoculars.

Pretty soon Dragonfly whispered, "Psst! Come here, Bill! Let's watch this spider eat her dinner!"

"I don't see any spider," I said, peeping into a hollow stump, both of us standing so our shadows wouldn't fall across it. I did see a nice new spider web stretched across one corner.

"Just wait," he said, and he showed me a fly he'd caught and was holding by its wings. He dropped the fly right into the middle of that sticky web, where it began to kick and squirm and get all tangled up. All spider webs are sticky, you know. That web bounced around and shook almost as much as Poetry's bed does when he turns over in his sleep.

"Psst!" Dragonfly said again.

Coming out of her hiding place was a little black spider, hurrying toward that fly.

"She's coming backwards!" I said, and sure enough she was. We couldn't see very well because we couldn't get close enough to look at her without scaring her away, and the binoculars wouldn't help. She was one of the smallest black spiders I'd ever seen, with kind of longish legs, yet not very long either.

Suddenly Dragonfly let out a gasp and jumped back so quick he bumped into me and almost knocked me down.

"What's the matter?" I said, not seeing anything to be so excited about.

"I—I *saw* it!" he exclaimed. "That reddish mark on her underneath side! She's a—a *black widow* spider!"

I tell you, Dragonfly was excited, and getting excited is contagious. I got excited too, and for a minute I was almost scared, although I knew we couldn't be bitten unless we were closer than we were.

You see, the black widow is a tiny black spider with a reddish mark on its stomach, shaped like an hourglass or else like a couple of triangles. It's about the most dangerous spider in the world, but there aren't very many of them, so boys don't need to be afraid of finding one every day. Of course, it's a good thing to kill any unknown spider you see around the house or cellar or anywhere, especially black ones.

Well, we got a couple of sticks and sneaked back to watch. And already that fly was fastened so tight in the web it could never have gotten away. Black widow spiders, you know, give off some kind of fluid that dries almost as quickly as rubber cement, and no fly or bug could get away even if it tried terribly hard.

In a flash the spider ran up to the fly as though she was terribly mad at it, and she must have bitten it for it started kicking and shaking harder than ever.

"It's dying!" Dragonfly said. "She's killing it!"

And sure enough, in a minute the fly was quiet, and Mrs. Spider was busy sucking on it as if she was sucking water through a straw.

"What'll we do?" Dragonfly said. "If it's a real black widow, it ought to be killed."

"It's the first one I ever saw," I said.

"And maybe the last one, although sometimes there are several together—especially if she's laid any eggs, and they've hatched."

We knew we would have been silly to poke around in that stump with our sticks trying to kill that spider. We might have gotten bitten ourselves.

My dad says if anybody gets bitten by a black widow, it might not even hurt at all at first, but pretty soon it will. And after a while you get sick to your stomach, and all your muscles down below your stomach get tight and hard, and you start sweating all over and maybe having a chill, and your skin starts to burn.

But if you do get bitten by one, you ought to put iodine on the bite real quick and have somebody get you to a doctor as soon as you can—awful soon, in fact. And be sure to tell him exactly what happened, so he'll know what to do for you.

Well, while we were standing there trying to decide what to do, we heard somebody coming. I looked up just in time to see a man dodging behind a tree, as though he was afraid that somebody would see him.

Dragonfly and I darted in back of some bushes and dropped down in the grass, wondering if it was one of the gang trying to sneak up on us.

Dragonfly had my binoculars. "I'll bet it's the robber!" he whispered, trying to be calm like Big Jim and to think what to do. "He must have gotten out of jail somehow and is running away," he said. "Maybe he's trying to hide down along the swamp again."

I guess my red hair must have stood right up on end when he told me. "Let's run!" I said.

We took off as fast as we could go, and we didn't stop until we had climbed clear up on top of the big hill where our gang meets sometimes. There we lay down behind the big rocks to get our wind, thinking maybe we'd better go on home quick and telephone for the sheriff again.

About that time, though, we thought we heard a car on the road not far from my house. Maybe the sheriff and his posse were already there. I took my binoculars and looked quick but didn't see anybody. And then I looked down toward the spring just in time to see a man come from behind a tree and go straight toward that old stump where we'd been not more than ten minutes ago.

He stopped at the stump, and Dragonfly nudged me and said, "What do you suppose he's doing there?"

"I don't know," I said, thinking, *What if he reaches inside?*

Just that minute, the man stood up quick with his head showing above the top of the stump, as though he was looking for something. But he seemed to be having a hard time finding what he wanted, and all the time I was scared he'd get bitten by that spider. We couldn't see very well, but it looked like the man had a gun. Now he climbed on top of the stump and was looking inside!

All of a sudden Dragonfly couldn't keep still any longer, for even if it was the robber, we didn't want him to get bitten. So Dragonfly screamed as though he was scared himself.

His scream was so loud and frightening that the man looked up. And then his foot slipped, and he fell inside the big stump.

I tell you I felt creepy all over, for I realized what might happen to him if that was a sure enough black widow spider in there. I thought the man had a gun and knew he was a desperate criminal and might shoot anybody he thought was after him. But as much as I wanted him to be caught, and knowing how wicked he was, I felt sorry for him. I kept thinking about what Little Jim would say and how he would feel if the man got bitten and had to die without letting Jesus into his heart.

"Let's go home quick!" I said to Dragonfly.

"Why?"

"I'm going to telephone for a doctor!"

"A *doctor!* What for?"

"Why, if he gets bit by that spider, and we don't get a doctor for him, he'll die!"

And then I was running as fast as I could toward our house, with Dragonfly right at my heels.

I didn't even take time to open our front gate, which opens hard anyway. I climbed over and ran up the walk, burst open the front door, and grabbed the telephone. Half a minute later I was talking to Dr. Gordon, our family doctor, with Mom and the nurse looking at me as though they thought I was crazy and telling me to keep still or I'd wake up Charlotte Ann.

"Quick, doctor!" I said into the telephone. "This is Bill Collins! Come out here quick and bring some iodine and whatever you need for a man who's been bit by a black widow spider!"

Then I hung up.

# 16

In about twenty minutes the doctor came, bringing another doctor with him. My dad had come home in the meantime, and we all went down through the woods toward the old hollow stump, and there we found the man lying on the grass.

He was all doubled up and sweating and trying to vomit. Just above his left eye was a swollen place about twice as big as a mosquito bite with two little red spots on it. And I guess I never was so surprised in my life when I saw who it was.

It wasn't the bank robber at all. *It was Circus's father!* And lying right beside him were three big whiskey bottles and his gun.

"Why, it's Dan Browne!" my dad cried. "I just took him home about an hour ago!"

Circus's dad rolled over and groaned. His arms and shoulders twitched. Then he saw my dad and looked scared. Between groans he said, "Honest, Mr. Collins! I wasn't going to . . . drink . . . it! I . . . had these bottles hid . . . here . . . and . . . and I came down to get them . . . I was goin' to put 'em up . . . on the stump and . . . and shoot 'em." Then he rolled over and groaned, staying all doubled up as if he had terrible cramps. "Spider!" he cried, pointing toward the stump. "Don't let the boys g-get b-bit!"

It didn't take the doctors long to put iodine on those little red spots to keep him from getting what they call "secondary infection." For just a minute they stood there talking, while Dragonfly and I watched and listened. And we heard a lot of long words that I didn't understand at the time but which I've since learned how to spell and pronounce because maybe someday I'm going to be a doctor myself.

The doctors decided to use a hypodermic and inject something right into one of his veins. Then they took Circus's father to the hospital as quick as they could, and my dad went with them.

Along about five o'clock in the afternoon, Dad came home, and I ran out to the car to meet him. He said they'd been careful to keep Mr. Browne as quiet as possible on the way, and in the hospital they gave him another shot in the muscles of his arm. "Convalescent serum," I think he said it was—which is made from the blood of somebody who's been bitten by a black widow spider and got well.

And then my dad just sat there behind the steering wheel for a while, not saying anything, so I climbed in beside him, Dragonfly having gone home about a half hour before.

He put his arm over the back of the car seat and let it touch my shoulder, as if he was not only my dad and I was his boy but we were real good friends. It felt good to have him do that. I just sat there thinking and wondering whether Circus's dad was going to live or not and also wanting to tell Dad I now knew for sure that I was saved.

"Well, Bill," Dad said, "Your quick action and presence of mind saved a life this afternoon."

That made me feel better. I felt proud to have him say that, but it didn't seem as important as something else just then, so I said, "Is— is Circus's dad saved yet?"

Dad looked at me quick to see if I really wanted to know, and I could feel his fingers tighten a little around my shoulder as if he liked me even better.

"No," he said. "I talked to him a long time at the jail, and he promised to be kind to his family and not get drunk anymore, but he would not accept Jesus into his heart."

"It'll be hard for him to be good without Jesus helping him, won't it?" I asked.

"Too hard," Dad said, "but he'll be in the hospital maybe a week, and he'll have time to think and read the Bible."

After a while, when Dad and I were doing the chores and I was in the haymow throwing down hay for the cows and horses, I climbed way up into the corner again. I took out my little New Testament and turned to one of the verses my mom had had me learn when I was little. I read it again just to be sure it really said what I thought it said and just to be certain I could know for sure I was saved.

This is what the verse said: "For God so loved the world, that He gave His only begotten Son, that whoever believes in Him should not perish, but have eternal life."

And then I *knew* I was saved, because God

says if I believe in Jesus (meaning with all my heart, of course) then I *have* everlasting life, and I wouldn't have to wait till I died to be sure I was going to heaven. I guess there isn't anything more wonderful than that, is there?

Then I got down on my knees and shut my eyes and said, "Dear Lord Jesus, I thank You for saving me. And for giving me such a nice little baby sister. And please help me to act like a Christian so other people will want to be saved too. And please help Circus's dad to see how much he needs You. And bless Little Jim and Poetry and Big Jim and Circus and Dragonfly and—and all the boys in the world."

I got up from my knees and put my New Testament back in the crack in the log, and I started whistling and throwing down more hay. I decided to leave my Bible there until Circus's dad was saved.

The next day some men came out from town and poured kerosene over that old hollow stump and set fire to it, so if there *were* any other black widow spiders there, or any eggs, they'd all be burned up. And do you know, we never did find any more of them in our neighborhood, even though we watched carefully for years.

But here I am, getting to the end of my story, and I haven't even told you about the time, about a month later, when Little Jim killed a black bear and maybe saved all of us from getting hurt. But that would make this story too long. Maybe if I have time, I'll tell you about it someday and a lot of other interesting things about the Sugar Creek gang and Old Man Paddler, and how Circus got his cornet, and how little Charlotte Ann grew and everything.

Anyway, the gang was all there while the men were burning that old stump. We lay in the tall grass not far from the creek, talking and laughing and having a good time watching the big yellow flames eat up that stump just like a hungry boy eating a big plateful of fried potatoes.

Even Circus seemed happy, because he knew his dad was going to get well. Pretty soon he jumped up and started climbing a little tree right behind us. He perched up there on a limb like a monkey, grinning and looking like the same old Circus again.

And while the flames leaped higher and higher and the blue and purple smoke rolled up in little cloud waves toward the sky, Poetry started quoting "America the Beautiful."

"Oh, beautiful, for spacious skies,
For amber waves of grain,
For purple mountain majesties
Above the fruited plain . . ."

Just then an old shitepoke went flying up the creek with its long, ugly neck sticking out in front of it like the long tongue on my green coaster wagon. I got out my binoculars and watched until it disappeared.

Finally we thought we'd watched the fire long enough, so we all jumped up and went down to the creek and went in swimming.